THIS TIME

Donna Ross Burchell

DAY ONE

"Rachel, slow down!" Joe Cokely shouted as he reached up to grab the safety handle on my Roush mustang.

I ignored him, like he wasn't a six-foot five giant sitting next to me. My mustang floated on the highway and it made my toes curl knowing that I was on the verge of losing control. I eased up on the pedal, still nearing 100mph, and felt the tires gain traction on the pavement. I glanced at him.

"I told you I wanted to drive back by myself."

"This shit has to stop. And I mean right now." He pounded his fist on the center console to make his point.

Annoyed, I downshifted through every gear and pulled to the side. We had spent the weekend clearing out my house in Myrtle Beach and handing the keys over to a Real Estate Agent. Overwhelmed with emotions, I couldn't bear anyone telling me one more thing I *had* to do.

"Joe, my dear husband, how about we call the guys to come get you? I haven't driven this car in months and it's exactly what Syncronia and I need. Get her fluids going, burn a little rubber, charge the battery. All that stuff."

Joe looked forward, not at me when I talked. His knees grazed the dashboard, even with the seat all the way back, and partially reclined so his head wouldn't hit the roof of my sports car. He looked pale but I doubted my driving scared my Navy SEAL, battle tested man.

"Do you want to die? Have you given up? Tell me where your head is at. I need you to tell me, Rae." Joe turned to me and placed his hand over mine, resting on the shifter.

"Christ, Joe, did it feel you like were going to die? Haven't you ever felt the urge, or actually needed to drive like that?"

I snatched my hand from under his. Rarely do I have a tone with him, but these three months of recuperation after getting shot in the stomach with non-stop attention and no privacy has driven me bonkers.

"I don't want to die, but I don't want to live in fear, either. Despite wanting to grow old with you, I think the odds for that are slim. We can both acknowledge that collecting coconuts on an island all day wouldn't fulfill us or bring us joy. Our life is full of danger. I've got a target on my back from an unknown number of psychos, the worst being Uncle Roger. Not recovering his body from the lake leads me to believe one thing. That his miserable soul is still alive. When he wants to, he'll come for me again. But I can't let him fill up my head space. I'm certainly not going to be afraid of doing whatever I want, even if it involves risk. Why should I? I could die tomorrow. Surely, as a soldier, you can comprehend that? Would you be happy in isolation just because it's safe? No, you wouldn't. I'll tell you every day, all day, I'd rather die by my own hand than Uncle Roger's. I'm sorry I scared you driving fast, but at least we'd die together."

He didn't laugh or even smile. Joe usually gets me, but it doesn't look like I'm registering with him.

Joe stared ahead for a minute before running his hand over his face. "Alright, my ride or die, let's go. They'll have to cremate the whole damn car if we crash, because they'll never get me out."

I checked my mirror and spun the tires getting back on the highway. I kept it at a reasonable speed most of the way back to camp, except on straight aways. His white knuckles from gripping the door showcased his dedication as a good husband.

We barely spoke, giving me ample time to think. I didn't realize I had any attachment to my house until we did a final walk through when it was empty. I was naïve to think a pretty house would help materialize a pretty life. It didn't. And the best thing that happened was Joe and FETCH kidnapped me from my garage last year. How crazy is that?

Seeking normalcy, I moved to South Carolina from New York. I thought I could start fresh. Yet, I brought an excessive amount of baggage. Watching my friends tortured and murdered changed me to my core. And what I did to my then husband and the four monsters who killed my friends changed my DNA. I realize that's not possible, but that's how deeply it affected me.

Joe is my saving grace. The more I thought about how much I loved him, the slower I drove. It would suck if we didn't get to grow old together. But that's life, at least mine. My parents got robbed of their longevity by my dad's brother, and he'll likely rob me of mine. Until he tried to kill me, I never even knew about him.

"Hey, let's stop at Popeye's and get lunch before we get back to camp."

Before I agreed, Joe called the team and told them we were stopping there.

"You know we have to eat there; I can't drive a stick and eat that chicken sandwich."

He draped his arm across the back of my seat and teased, "Yeah, that would surely cause my death."

Back at camp, we unloaded my car and an SUV full of my belongings. They couldn't understand why I needed all my shoes, sneakers and boots. I just do, I told them, as well as needing a crap ton of clothes I'll never wear again. My prerogative.

I stayed upstairs trying to organize my clothes for the rest of the day until dinner time. I ought to have tossed these clothes already. But I needed more time to say goodbye to the me that wore them. Before I was FETCH. The short party dresses didn't fit my personality, but they sure helped when I was picking up one-night stands. It feels like ages ago, and incredibly foolish.

In the two years following the incident, I explored various paths, attempting to discover my true self, and occasionally evading the person I recognized myself to be. I am my parent's daughter, who unbeknownst to me, trained me all my life to be a resilient warrior. I can own that now. I'm proud to be a member of FETCH: For the Education and Training of Civilian Hostages. After what happened to me, there wasn't a more perfect job for me.

After sorting, I ended up with a bag full of skimpy clothes. I wonder what kind of shelter would take this stuff?

These big boys I live with never miss a meal, so I cruised downstairs around five to see what the plan was. Rocky Roberts was making hamburger patties to grill on this beautiful day in March. I walked around the bar top and asked if he needed help.

"No, we moved the fryer to the porch so the house doesn't smell. Thought we'd keep it simple tonight."

I opened the fridge, grabbed a beer, and ventured out to the porch.

Joe, Dusty Lockwood, and Alex Schinski were sitting in rockers, Bobby Bridges and Mickey Deans sat on the steps and Eddie Powers leaned against the railing. I propped up near Eddie and looked out past all our buildings. This is our haven, where we can relax and drop our defenses. The guys don't worry about someone trying to kill me here either. Mostly, I've stopped questioning why it all happened to me because that only leads to victim mentality and I'm not that. I was a victim of a horrible crime, but I don't identify as that circumstance. I remember the words of the old vets I met when I first came here - they called me a warrior. I hope to be one until the day I die.

Joe broke me out of my musing with an announcement. "I talked with my father and told him we're all good to go, ready for an assignment, and he sent over the file for our next case. The guy lives in New Orleans and had a pretty harrowing experience during Mardi Gras. He needs us to go over his operation from head to toe."

Turning his body, Bobby inquired, "What kind of operation does he have down there?"

Joe hesitated, snickered, and said, "He's in the entertainment industry. He's unique."

Alex said, "Well, that sets off all kinds of red flags for me."

Rocky brought the burgers out and delayed us hearing about our new case. Once he had them arranged on the grill, Joe continued.

"A career-ending knee injury derailed his NFL first-round draft pick prospects. He turned to rap music and fell in with the wrong crowd. He's got a police sheet but never got arrested. He finally hit a low point and turned his life around, forming new friendships and creating new music. Now he's in the genre of blues-country music."

"Oh, for fuck's sake." I couldn't help myself.

Eddie elbowed me and said, "I thought you gave up cussing."

Joe finally lowered his eyebrow and said, "A few weeks ago he started getting death threats. He hired a bunch of old teammates thinking because of their size it would scare people off, but that hasn't worked. They lack security training beyond intimidating smaller individuals and are clueless about handling threats."

Mickey told Rocky, "I want mine rare, so keep track of it, please."

Rocky tapped his watch and said, "It'll be perfect, don't you worry." He loaded a batch of fries into the fryer and we waited until it stopped hissing for Joe to continue.

Joe suggested that Mickey print out the file for everyone after dinner so we can put a plan together. I turned around and chugged the rest of my beer. I shouldn't act like I already hate the guy because he sings country music. I'm still friends with our client Cash Black and he's really country. I need to keep an open mind. I don't have to like everyone to help them.

Rocky declared dinner ready and plated the burgers. Dusty emptied the second batch of fries on to a plate and we all went inside to eat. Mickey took his plate and sat in front of his computer. Seconds later, he was printing the new file. Curiosity was killing me, so I grabbed the first copy and sat at the table. The rest waited for Mickey to finish printing and hand them out, and we ate while reading the file.

Eddie said, "Oh man, I remember him. They took the film of his injury off media because it was so gruesome. Worse than anyone I've ever seen, for sure."

Mickey said, "Let me try to find it," and turned back to his computer.

Alex said, "Look at his stats. He was a beast. Definitely a number one round draft pick."

I focused on a photo, but not the football picture. He was possibly the most handsome black man I'd ever seen, all six foot seven of him. He looks to have lost about fifty pounds from his football days, now he's cut like granite. The photo showed him onstage, shirtless, wearing low rider jeans. He was a pretty man with a hard edge.

Bobby started reading out loud. "Strong family history in law enforcement and military. They rejected him from both jobs after his injury because of the metal in his leg. It's enough to make you go in the opposite direction. Now, he expresses his patriotism in the only way he can. Gotta give him credit for that, big time."

Joe asked, "You guys want to go tomorrow or the next day? It's about a ten-hour drive, unless Rachel drives." He winked at me.

Alex asked, "Why don't we split the trip up? Then we don't have to hurry tomorrow morning." We all nodded in agreement. I doubted if any of his football buddies would listen to my advice, but we'll find out.

Mickey found the film of his injury to watch, then pulled up many more of athletes getting injured. It amazed me when they all groaned because I knew they'd seen much worse in combat. I guess they were good at compartmentalizing their military life vs civilian life, sports vs IEDs. We watched the tapes until it was time for bed.

DAY TWO

"Here ya go, Rae." Joe put my coffee on the bedside table and kissed my cheek. I grabbed his hand as he stood up from me.

"Why don't you give me about five minutes and come back?" I wiggled my eyebrows and smiled at him. "We get so busy on the road."

Joe put his finger to my lips. "Say no more, babe. I'll be right back." I drank my coffee as fast as possible while I freshened up and was back in bed when he returned. A half hour later, we joined the team downstairs.

Dusty asked, "Everyone packed? I'll start loading the cars."

Every one of us had a duffle bag with our initials by the door. The four extra bags and two long gun cases were new. They weren't traveling light after what happened last time. I wish it made me feel safer.

Bobby said, "We've got all our inventions with us to add to our personal security. It'll be ok."

He must have thought I was having second thoughts or was afraid. He'd freak out if he thought I wasn't scared anymore. He might even think I was dangerous. Bobby was our psych guy and sometimes he was too good at his job when you wanted to keep secrets.

Joe proposed having breakfast on the go to avoid cleaning up here. We took three vehicles this time to accommodate all of our gear. Joe and I rode alone in the second SUV. We stopped at the Bojangles drive thru to get bags of food and continued southwest to our first stop near Montgomery, Alabama.

I read Joe all the information on who our client, Nate Graham had surrounding him. The weakest link was the poorest guy. He'd be the one to sell out if someone flashed enough money in front of him. He never made it to the NFL because of his bad habits, but he and Nate were roomies in college, so I guess he thought he owed him? The remaining five had little going for them either, making them available to Nate.

Joe said, "Don't worry, we'll put them to the test before we waste time training them."

We stopped for dinner before we found a hotel that met our standards. Which meant they had security and lots of cameras. Joe called a meeting after we got checked in.

"Alright, I think we need to observe who we're dealing with before they see us. Test their loyalty and their strengths. Rachel will be the first one to test if she can crack someone."

I gave him a strange look, wondering why he didn't mention this during our six-hour car ride alone.

He failed to notice and suggested, "Just pretend you're interested in Nate and see if they let you get close. He'll be performing downtown and that alone can be a nightmare. We'll have to watch Rachel and the crowd."

Eddie stated he's okay as long as he has a good sightline. The guys looked like they wanted to question Joe's plan.

I insisted, "Listen up, guys. I'm not living the rest of my life in a bubble. I can't. I have a target on my back from more than one person, but I can't let it dictate how I live. I've made peace with checking out early. While I'm here, I aim to make an impact and ensure my life has meaning. I don't want you guys feeling responsible if anything happens. I know you'd do anything for me. I'm asking you to treat me as part of the team, not a damsel in distress."

It's doubtful they'll perceive me in such a manner. I'm certainly not equal to them. I want to spare them guilt if something happens to me. If something does, it's certainly my fault.

Joe waited a beat and said, "We're going to approach what we've deemed the weakest link and offer him a bribe to get Nate to a location for us. We'll decide our course of action after that."

Alex filled us in on the culture of New Orleans, having been there for Mardi Gras a couple of times. The bars weren't huge, but standing shoulder to shoulder to watch a band was normal. The saying should be what happens in New Orleans stays in New Orleans instead of Vegas. People lose their minds, morals and inhibitions there. He added, "Oh, it smells like vomit and urine just about everywhere you go."

I longed for a good rock-n-roll band at an outside arena in upstate New York. We discussed the events and bars in New Orleans before the guys left our room. We planned to meet at 7:00am by the vehicles.

Joe stood behind me in the bathroom, looking over my head in the mirror. He touched my shoulders and admitted, "You don't understand the difficulty of intentionally putting you in harm's way. That's why I've been pushing you so hard in training. I know you've survived the hardest days of your life without my help, but I feel responsible for you, as my wife and part of the team I'm in charge of. You know Eddie is the best marksman of anyone I know. He has records for it and he's made himself crazy for not taking the kill shot on Roger. We all react a little different with you, and I've told them all it has to change. You deserve more credit for staying alive and being resourceful. You don't need to be coddled. You're one of us."

To know that my husband had confidence in my ability gave me more courage. For him, as a man, a skilled Navy SEAL, to relinquish a bit of control over me was a big deal, and if I didn't earn that respect, he wouldn't give it. I turned and slowly unbuttoned his pants, and told him I'd show him how happy I was that he felt that way. His knees were shaking in minutes.

DAY THREE

We were on the road at 7:05am, final destination, New Orleans. I rode with Eddie and Alex today; Bobby took my place with Joe. After covering a few miles on the road, Eddie mentioned, "I understand that we have already gone through this, but now that we have a clear idea of our direction, let's focus on the different situations we might encounter."

I said, "Eddie, for the thousandth time, it's not your fault. I got in the way."

He countered, "Ok, listen up. You should always think that I'm somewhere with a bead on you. Keep your head low if you're near a target, if they have you in a headlock, become deadweight to make the space between your head and theirs bigger. When you see my red dot, get away from my target if you can. And don't be spastic moving around. I don't need two moving targets." He was on a roll. "If someone holds a gun to your head, try to insert your finger into the firearm to prevent them from firing."

Alex finally contributed by saying, "These bars are so crowded that a dead person could stand for another five minutes before he fell. So, if the shit hits the fan, get low, get to a wall, and if you're near the bar, jump it. Besides your own weapons, you might find some non-lethal weapons back there, a fire extinguisher or even throwing full bottles of liquor will put a hurting on someone."

As Alex talked, I envisioned what he was saying and playing out a worst-case scenario in my head. I didn't want to be the weakest link on my team. Alex kept me alive until they got me to the hospital when my uncle shot me. I clearly trust him with my life.

We chatted occasionally over the next few hours and listened to the hard rock station Octane on the radio. My imagination was working hard as I looked at the terrain we'd be crossing when I told them, "Just so you're aware, if we crash into a swamp, you're on your own. I will literally walk over your bodies to get out. Not playing."

They cracked up and said, "Noted".

We were staying at a mansion, much to my surprise, and not a hotel. Behind the immense brick house was a small parking lot, with a skinny driveway between houses to navigate. Shrubbery that I'd never seen surrounded the lot to give it some privacy. An older man awaited us at the back door as we grabbed our bags.

Joe greeted him warmly and said, "Nice to see you, sir."

The man greeted Joe the same way. "Glad to see you, Joseph. Let's get you all inside and settled."

We exchanged glances. Guess he didn't tell anyone he knew this guy. The man showed us to our rooms, then invited us downstairs for a drink.

"I have to use the bathroom first." Joe sat on the bed waiting for me. When I came out, I said, "Let me guess, a friend of your dad's?"

Joe stood and acknowledged that and said he knew my dad, too. I hurried downstairs to see him, skipping two steps at a time. He was pouring liquor and pointing to the fridge for those that wanted beer. They were introducing themselves and giving their special ranks.

He shifted his attention towards me as I made my not so graceful entrance and reached out his hand. "Pleasure to meet you, Rachel. JD tells me you're a chip off the old block. Your father would be proud of how resilient you are."

I made a funny face to hold back my tears. In a cracked voice, I said, "Thank you for saying that. I hope he would be. I assume you knew him in the Army?"

He smiled and said, "In another world."

He was vague about his past and no one pushed it. I guessed Frank to be in his seventies, judging by the wrinkles on his face, but his tall, lean figure moved like a younger man.

Frank was aware of what FETCH was doing and showed us a map of the Bourbon Street area. He pointed out narrow alleys we could travel to avoid or evade the crowd. He disclosed bars with back door access for quick get-aways.

"It's very hard to find a good vantage point here. Standing on the balcony provides a view of the street, excluding the people below. If you want to stay hidden, you walk next to the buildings, even if that means stepping over people sitting on the sidewalk leaning against buildings. You'll get around best on foot."

Joe checked his watched and said Nate would be here any minute. As if on cue, we heard a loud rumble sneaking between the houses to park in the lot. Joe met him at the back door and led him in. Dressed in track gear, he was even better looking in person. He expressed his genuine appreciation for our help and was open and friendly. Why would anyone want to kill him? He said he hoped we enjoyed his show tonight, and he'd see us after.

Dusty asked, "What bar are we going to tonight?" Joe pointed to the bar, and I studied the area.

Frank advised, "If you're alone in there, you're alone. Nothing is visible from the outside. The back door and upstairs provide extra ways to access the area. Nate Graham has been performing for over a month. He packs them in, shoulder to shoulder."

No one said anything. They were just breathing loudly and thinking.

I assured them, "I'll be fine. I'll be on coms, right?"

Mickey said, "Of course."

"Ok, if I get uncomfortable, I'll let you know, and you can all storm the place and save me."

Frank smirked as he looked around.

Joe stretched his neck and asked, "Where's the best place to get dinner?"

Frank suggested getting true gumbo and oyster poor boys at his favorite place. Alex mentioned wanting rabbit and sausage jambalaya, and Rocky insisted on getting oysters. Based on Frank's opinion, the offerings of New Orleans would bring satisfaction to all of us.

Joe said, "Let's get changed and loaded. We'll set up around the bar after we eat."

I put one of our newly designed mesh shirts over a bandeau bathing suit top with jeans and my cowboy boots that held a knife in each boot. My belt came apart at the buckle and held a knife. The middle stud on the buckle was a camera. Just a few things we made recently. Joe sat on the bed watching me. "I'm fine with this, it'll be ok." I tried to reassure him, but he kept scowling.

"I know you'll be ok, but I don't like it, and I never will, but I trust your ability to handle yourself. So, let's go."

We walked about twelve blocks through the streets and the noise and crowd increased the closer we got to Bourbon Street. Every few feet, a unique aroma wafted in front of us;

seafood, spices, meats, body odors, alcohol and sweets. We reached the place Frank suggested, but there was a wait, so we kept walking. We stopped to read a few menus and split off in twos at different eateries, hoping to be served faster.

After dinner we rejoined and walked to the bar, another few blocks away, marching along with young tourists and dodging lone musicians hoping to fill their buckets with donations. The crowd seemed to get younger and drunker the further we walked. They stumbled into the street and over cracks in the sidewalk but kept forging down Bourbon Street to their destinations. A band of bridesmaids intercepted Bobby and Alex briefly, trying to recruit them as a present for the bride. Can't blame them. All the guys were over six feet, muscled, tattooed, and handsome.

When we arrived at the busy Hanky Tank, Joe stopped me before I stepped inside by myself. "Don't let any of these drunks grope you."

I was laughing as I walked inside and shimmied up to the bar for a beer. I had to turn away because of the armpit odor from the guy next to me, mixed with the alcohol and spicy smell of food had me gagging, especially on a full stomach. My breath would hold its own in a fight, though, I'm sure, after the muffuletta I ate.

I looked around for Nate's security, but didn't spot anyone resembling a football player. Without a barrier, the band's instruments sat on a stage barely a foot off the floor, close to the audience. I highly doubted anyone could stop an attack in here. It was impossible to see anyone's hands; the lighting was dim and people did indeed stand shoulder to shoulder. I hoped the threats he was getting were empty ones, because in this venue he would be hard to protect. I debated on getting another beer before trying to get closer to the stage when I caught sight of three of his so-called security push their way to the bar. They started with shots and continued with another round of them. Granted, they were big guys, but it didn't appear as though they were taking the threats seriously enough to stay sober for tonight's gig. The guy we deemed the weakest link came out to stand with them at the bar and my focus shifted to him and his searching eyes. His eyes kept moving toward the stage, but his head didn't move.

The camera on my belt was useless in here, except to get booty shots of whoever stood in front of me. With my beer raised to my face, to cover my mouth, I told them to keep watch on the stage's far side. "The weakest link keeps glancing over there and acting like he wants to be somewhere else."

Within seconds, a redhead, moving swiftly, appeared above the crowd. Rocky cleared a path to the front. The weak link fidgeted with his beer label and pretended to listen to the other three.

Rocky's voice vibrated in my ear. "Everybody in."

Oh hell, what was happening? The team, minus Eddie, arrived a few seconds apart and filtered themselves throughout the bar. Joe walked past me at the bar and pushed his way in until he stood next to the football players. Dusty moved to the opposite side. They were oblivious to their surroundings, and the weakest link continued looking for someone by the stage.

Rocky chimed in again, pointing out a guy with a bulge around his waist. "Black t-shirt, stout, bald."

The lights flickered to announce the beginning of the show as Nate Graham walked on stage. The girls in the crowd pushed their way forward to get a better view. His bodyguards barely turned around, demonstrating exactly how worthless they all were. The female fans swooning over the singer captured the attention of the two supposed security guards positioned by the stage. Bobby noticed two guys who didn't belong amidst the girls in the front. The crowd was more black than white and single, beefy, white bald guys didn't seem to be the typical fan of Nate Graham.

In my ear, "Rachel, you're up. Go check those two guys for weapons. I'll be close."

I nearly got in a cat fight with scantily clothed groupies trying to get closer. I deliberately bumped into the first guy I came to and then put my arms around him to steady myself. Apologizing, I put my hands up on his shoulders, then ran them down his chest to his waist. He didn't seem to have a weapon, so I moved on. I tried to dance my way to the other guy, but moving was difficult. I legit plowed into him and he didn't like it. He turned, jabbing his finger into my chest, demanding that I step back. Wrong move, buddy. I grabbed his index finger with my left hand and his pinky with my right hand and pulled them apart as far as I could. I kicked him in the shin and shoved him backwards, but there wasn't any room for him to fall or even lose his balance. He grabbed my hand and pried it off his finger, and pushed me back. The person behind me pushed me forward, not knowing what was going on.

Rocky appeared behind him and de-armed him of a gun and knife without the guy noticing until Rocky grabbed his right arm and torqued it behind his back. He then restrained the guy's left hand behind his back and zip-tied his wrists. He struggled against Rocky until I stomped his foot as hard as I could. Bobby slid next to him and grabbed one side while Rocky lifted him up on the other side. While bulldozing through the crowd, two other white bald guys tried to stop them. They had limited wind up in their punches and didn't slow the guys down. And the crowd sang along with Nate, oblivious.

The music stopped abruptly; the microphone reverberated from being dropped, and metal clashed. Yelling replaced the music, and I saw flashes of people dashing across the stage. Joe rushed Nate off the stage and the band members followed them. Dusty and Alex were nearing us when the first gunshot rang out. Shit. Que chaos.

Rocky's big hand reached in back of him and pushed my head down. The two guys that tried to free their friend vanished into the crowd. I tucked myself up tight and darted to the wall so I wouldn't get trampled. Amidst two more shots, people screamed and pushed toward the exit. I pulled my pants up out of the way and grabbed both knives from my boots. Most of the crowd was trying to exit while I tried to spot anyone coming into the bar. Rocky, Bobby and Dusty pushed back towards the stage and Alex followed me.

The bar cleared itself by the sheer will to survive. People inside rushed past those on the street, fleeing from the bar. In a few minutes, the only people in the bar were FETCH, the bartenders, Nate's band members, his security, and the bad guys. The five bad guys were either subdued or wounded. Apparently, they were pretty bad shots because no one else was hurt. It was silent, except for the blood rush in my ears.

While still backstage with Nate, Joe asked us to check in on coms. I said my name first so he could focus instead of worrying about me.

One bartender yelled the police were on the way. The supposed bodyguards looked scared to death and the weak link wasn't in the bar. Dusty instructed them to watch over the three on the floor while Alex examined the leg wounds of the other two. They shouldn't have kept their fingers on the trigger when they were fighting the big boys and shot themselves. Joe emerged with Nate by his side and directed the band members to wait backstage.

Nate glared at his guys and asked, "What the fuck am I paying you for? And where's WV?"

The weak link was from West Virginia, so I assumed that's who he meant. Bursting through the door, a man waved a gun around, clearly inexperienced. His eyes darted around, searching for someone or a target. I still had my knives in my hand and sent one sailing toward him, distracting him before he fired. Then Alex rushed him and probably gave him a concussion from the sound of his head hitting the floor. Game over for that guy.

Nate walked around with his hands rubbing his head, mumbling to himself and occasionally glancing around. Joe guided him to the stage, instructing him to sit and pay attention.

One of his bodyguards approached him and he screamed, "Get the fuck away from me, man."

The New Orleans Police arrived and were none too happy surveying the scene, with two guys bleeding on the floor, holding their wounds. They drew their guns and yelled too many directions at once to us. Joe stepped forward and introduced himself, with his hands on his head, just to be safe. I was afraid they were going to shoot one of us before they calmed down. Rocky put his fingers in his mouth and performed a shrilling whistle to shut everyone up. The police noticed the crowd now gathering outside and slammed the doors to the onlookers.

Despite our compliance and raised hands, one of them frantically barked at us to line up at the bar. Joe politely asked who was in charge, but the smallest napoleon confronted him, demanding obedience. "I'll ask the questions. Do as I say."

Nate stood up from the stage and started walking toward us and was warned he'd to be tased if he didn't stop moving. He introduced himself as the entertainer tonight, but they didn't care who he was. It scared me that the police hadn't de-escalated yet, but then I looked around at the mountains I was with, including Nate, and thought they were probably being extra cautious. While most of the team conversed with other officers, the Napoleon officer targeted Nate and began provoking him.

I slowly made my way over to Nate and stood in front of him, facing him. "Don't move and don't take your hands off your head. And don't say a word."

He angled his head down to me to acknowledge what I said and stood straight up to his full height, and closed his eyes. The officer told me to move away from Nate and grabbed my arm, pointing his gun at me. The room fell silent.

Joe warned, "Get your gun out of her face and stand down."

He squeezed my arm harder and asked Joe, "What are you going to do about it?"

Finally, another officer's voice of reason advised him to lower his weapon and stand down. This guy was waving his gun around between me and Nate. Joe and the guys had all lowered their arms and were inching toward us. Joe signaled to the officers, warning them to control him. The officers kept shouting at him as Joe crept closer. I was getting nervous. I didn't want to experience being shot again. The officer appeared eager to fire his weapon.

I gestured to Nate, indicating for him to hold the cop's arm up in the air, away from us. "Now."

Nate loomed over him and grabbed his arm, nearly picking the guy off the floor. Joe and Bobby rushed forward and got him on the ground and used his own handcuffs on him while the other officers watched with their guns out. I stood back and glanced at Nate, who stood with his fists clenched, ready to pounce and kick the shit out of this guy.

I told him, "Back it up, big guy. Not worth it." He stared down at the man until I yelled, "Nate! Back up."

A high-ranking officer arrived, as well as Frank and the room suddenly became calm. The officer looked confused when he saw one of his men in handcuffs.

An officer nodded his head in confirmation and he ordered, "Take those men and Officer Dodge into custody."

They dragged the officer off, kicking and screaming like he was the victim.

Joe positioned himself in front of me and Nate with his arms crossed and feet wide. He was an impenetrable wall. Nate realized the napoleon officer was in on the plot against him and it was his undoing. The giant man started crying. It was difficult to determine if it was frustration or anger.

Bobby declared he would bring Nate backstage, where they would remain until necessary.

Frank and the officer surveyed the damage and men on the floor. Chief Bogart introduced himself and questioned the necessity of it all, adding that discharging firearms in the city was illegal. "I'd like a quick summary of the situation so we can proceed with charging the responsible parties."

Joe stepped forward and offered his hand. "Joe Cokely, team leader. The two wounded discharged their own weapons. We did what was necessary to save Nate's life."

The chief mentioned confiscating our weapons and detaining everyone until they resolve the situation.

Joe replied quickly, "Will we be joining your officer that was involved in a plot to murder our client?"

Frank stepped forward and offered, "I can vouch for the team. They'll cooperate fully with your investigation."

Bogart narrowed his eyes at Frank before he said, "Sure, stay in town. We'll be in touch." Bogart must have trusted Frank to change his attitude so quickly.

The door opened for the ambulance crew. They paused at the door to survey the scene and awaited Bogart's signal. Detectives arrived to question the band and the bartenders, who stated the wounded guys were the ones to shoot. It's unclear how they reached that conclusion, but they were adamant about it. It also helped that they shot themselves with their own weapons after they drew on FETCH. Bogart threw a thank you toward us hours later before we left and walked back to Frank's house.

Bobby informed us that Nate was taking a break from performing. Tonight proved too overwhelming for him and he struggled to make sense of the entire situation.

I agreed. "I totally get that. This shit is very overwhelming."

Frank was sitting in the front room of his house, which he called the parlor. He motioned for us to join him.

He said, "I think it's best if you head out-of-town tomorrow. I'll handle any follow up with the department for you."

He gave us our eviction notice.

Joe said, "I'm sorry if your affiliation with us caused you any trouble. We'll leave our contact numbers with you and clear out in the morning." He stood and Frank did too.

Frank said, "I think you misunderstood me. You're no trouble for me, and this isn't over. Another agency will investigate the department and the plot against Nate. Your work is complete, no need to expose yourselves unnecessarily."

Joe relaxed and said, "We'll be available whenever you need us. Thanks for all your help."

Frank offered, "I've got a fresh supply of liquor if you'd all care to join me."

We couldn't say no. Frank poured and handed us each a glass. He winked at me when he handed me mine.

I asked, "Is this going to grow hair on my chest, Frank?"

He snickered, "It's possible, my dear."

He raised his glass to the room and said, "Salute."

We all replied the same. The tiny sip I took made me shudder and my eyes water. Frank was watching me and smiled. The guys relaxed and drank their fire water and recounted the night for Frank. We moved on and talked about new equipment helping in ways Frank wished he had when he was 'working'. The sun was coming up when we finally called it a night. We agreed to be ready to leave by noon.

DAY FOUR

Frank saw us off with bags of New Orleans beignets and plenty of napkins for all the powdered sugar that lined the bags. He also gave us a cooler full of king cake, Doberge layered cake, and sweet and sugary pecan pralines. We made a deal that the keeper of the cooler wouldn't eat the contents before we made our next stop.

I was glad to have met Frank. Despite any of my dad's associates having much to say, they believed he would be proud of me. Although they didn't talk about his work or personal matters, meeting them was meaningful, as they shared a connection with a part of my dad that was unknown to me. It was beyond anyone's capacity to categorize the extent of his impact on this country, but it was universally acknowledged that he was unmatched in his field.

Mickey's voice came through the comms, five miles down the road, announcing new orders. "Set your GPS to Jensen Beach, Florida. I'll send everyone the file to peruse on the way."

Rocky asked, "Peruse? What the hell, Mickey."

Joe scrolled the file and said, "Hey, looks like we'll be staying with Uncle Jim at the old folks' home." Chuckling, he shared how his uncle and aunt owned a place at a resort for people aged 55 and above. It was for the rich, early retired people, not frail elders. "We can be ourselves during the visit as we investigate peculiar occurrences. Could be nothing, could be something."

I pretended to sleep while I replayed the last few days in my head. I tried to talk myself into believing the bullshit I told the guys about my new life motto and wondered if they bought it? I needed to because I don't have a choice. No one emerges unharmed from the eye of a hurricane. That's where I lived now, in the storm with my incredible husband and teammates, and that's probably where I'll die. At least I'll have mattered.

After a few pit stops, we got hotel rooms on 1A near Jensen Beach around midnight. After tonight, Joe and I would stay at the resort with Jim and Char.

DAY FIVE

Joe was on the phone with his father when I woke up. It seems retired General JD Cokely was having second thoughts of us being so close to relatives and putting them at risk of being a target. Joe paced as he talked and said, "I won't try to reassure you. You either trust us or you don't. Your call." His father's raised voice filled the room, even as Joe pressed the phone to his ear tighter and walked in bigger circles around the room. Joe ended the call by saying, "We'll be over there in an hour and keep you in the loop. Goodbye, General."

"Joe, that was pretty formal calling him that. What's up? I thought Uncle Jim asked for us? Does JD believe I'm too dangerous to associate with now?"

Joe spun around. "No, it's not you. He thinks Uncle Jim is getting too involved and needs to be reeled in, and isn't sure I can wield that authority over him. Said he thinks he's a 007 suddenly."

I laughed and said, "I bet Aunt Charlotte likes that, spices things up a bit." Joe shook his head and walked into the bathroom to take a shower.

An hour later, Joe and I pulled into Oceanside Breeze and waited to be buzzed into the resort. We drove by million-dollar motor coaches as we crawled through the park en route to an elevated aqua sided house. It sat at the end of a row with other brightly colored houses that edged the moveable homes. Under the house sat a matching-colored golf cart that was covered in shamrocks and green tinsel for St. Patrick's Day and a new white Ford pickup. Our SUV pulled under to park too.

Uncle Jim and Aunt Char practically ran down the steps to greet us. Uncle Jim looked past us, questioning the whereabout of the rest of the team because he needed all hands-on deck. He definitely seemed eager.

Joe said, "Oh, they're around. But we have to keep it low key to avoid the attention."

"Good thinking," He replied.

Joe grabbed our bags and we climbed the stairs to the house. The space, around 1200 square feet, felt surprisingly open and larger than expected. Aunt Char pointed to our room and asked if we had eaten breakfast yet. I said we hadn't, and she suggested we walk to a restaurant down the street.

Uncle Jim said, "Good idea. That way I can give you the lay of the land. The details, the ins and outs of the resort."

Joe rolled his eyes at me and said, "Let's do it."

We used the cut-through sidewalks to leave the resort and get to Jensen Beach Road. We crossed the street to find a seat outside the bistro to eat. Joe put his phone on speaker for the team to hear the conversation. His uncle talked nonstop, except when the waitress was near, about his theories and plans to find the culprits who were vandalizing their winter sanctuary. He mentioned people sensed they were being watched, and a few had peculiar personal items stolen from their RVs. It sounded like it was too sophisticated for kids pulling pranks, but the villains weren't professionals either.

Mickey called during our walk back and mentioned bringing portable cameras to the resort. He was also running a list of all the guests registered here and the surrounding neighborhoods within five miles to see if anyone jumped out.

"Could it just be some young punks looking to bother the rich old folks?" Uncle Jim almost tripped on the sidewalk when he turned to look at me and my ridiculous statement.

Joe said, "We'll figure it out. No theory is off limits right now."

Opting for a longer path, we meandered beside the Indian River, which separates us from the ocean, until we reached the resort's entrance. They gave us a tour of the amenities that included an enormous pool, clubhouse, gym and pickle ball courts. It was a high-class place for people that wintered here in their expensive motor coaches. There were signs up announcing St Patty's Day celebrations throughout the resort and sign-up sheets for attending.

Mickey and Bobby met us at the house after having walked through the neighborhood. They had already positioned two cameras along the route.

Mickey said, "They're just stick on, battery operated, so they can go anywhere, and we can all access them on our phones."

Aunt Char announced it was her time for pickle ball, grabbed her racket and left. Uncle Jim reminded us where the incidents happened and we planned where the other cameras should go.

It took us almost two hours to nonchalantly place the cameras because we kept getting stopped by the friendly but nosey residents. The silver sneaker neighborhood watch was out in force. Later, we strolled to a large Irish restaurant on the second floor. The guys were there, sitting in twos at different tables, watching the crowd.

Aunt Charlotte had enough of the spy talk and ordered the largest size margaritas for her and me so I couldn't object.

With both hands, she lifted the frosty glass, giggled while licking the salt, then took a big gulp. The place filled with resort patrons, who waved or stopped to say hello. The older women ogled Joe, and several had the nerve to rub his muscled shoulder and introduced themselves. He ate it up.

Alex sent a text to check out the three guys near the bathroom. Nothing about them was remarkable, yet they seemed off. They looked grungy, had half glasses of water in front of them, and they weren't eating. Alex noticed they seemed to have an interest in a couple at the bar. Facing them, I noticed their frequent glances towards the couple.

Aunt Char mentioned the couple was new to the resort, whereas she and Jim were regulars for four years and knew nearly everyone. While en route to the bathroom, she stopped and engaged in a lengthy conversation with the couple. When she came back, she told us their names, and they were from Vestal, New York, then said, "Can you google that?" She laughed and ordered another drink.

Uncle Jim touched her shoulder proudly and whispered, "Good job, darling."

I informed them, "Vestal is my neck of the woods, near Binghamton."

Mickey messaged back with the couple's licenses and they were who they said they were. Now to find out why they held the trio's interest. We decided that Rocky and Dusty would follow the couple and Bobby and Alex would follow the three guys. Eddie kept his eyes on us, and Mickey worked his computer skills and kept watch on the cameras.

We stayed at the bar as long as possible, but the couple outlasted everyone, even the guys near the bathroom. They left, along with Rocky and Dusty. The four of us left next, Eddie followed, and Mickey headed to the SUV to keep working on the computer. Rocky sent the license number of the van the guys were driving and said it headed away from the beach, but they couldn't follow because of a train crossing.

Joe called everyone and directed them to walk through the resort and come to the house. Mickey linked up Uncle Jim's computer to all the cameras, so it was easier to watch all the action on two larger screens. An hour later, the first street camera blinked activity as the couple at the bar staggered down the street to their coach.

With a coconut drink in her hand, the woman's balance wavered as they turned onto a street without cameras. Another sensor tripped a camera, so we switched to watch that. With a flashlight, two men huddled by a fence, rummaging through a duffle bag. They stood and put something small into their pockets and walked down a street without a camera, but we recognized them from the bar, minus one friend.

There was a commotion on the street near ours. Onlookers gathered in the street, observing the woman from the bar, yet her husband was absent. Aunt Char had passed out on the couch, her mouth agape and snoring loudly. Uncle Jim, Joe, and I rushed downstairs to investigate. The team snaked their way around the streets to find the two grungy guys.

Joe elbowed his way through the group of people standing over her to check her pulse. She was alive, but he couldn't rouse her. "Has someone called 911 yet?"

"Yes!" a woman answered. "And we urged them to hurry."

Someone trying to get a closer look accidentally bumped me into the person ahead. He reached behind himself to check his weapon. He turned around and said, "Don't worry, miss, I never leave home without it."

I pulled up my shirt and said, "Me either."

He smiled, reached his hand to me and said, "I'm Fred. Nice to meet you. This is my wife, Deb, if you need anything while you're here."

Deb smiled at me, then redirected her attention to the woman on the ground. I wonder if they were acquainted with Uncle Jim? They seemed like they'd get along, being gun-toting camo-croc wearers.

The ambulance crew arrived and asked bystanders for any information on this poor woman as they started an IV and gave her oxygen. Paramedics received another call about a man falling into the river before they left our scene. They loaded the coconut head lady in their rig and sped away. Joe and I held hands as we sauntered off in the river's direction, leaving Uncle Jim to gossip with his neighbors.

We crossed the street and stood with a larger crowd of onlookers as the EMTs hauled the husband out of the water and onto a gurney. He was a bloody mess, seemingly from head to toe. I couldn't tell if he'd been shot, beaten, or what had happened to him. I looked over the edge to at least a 10ft fall onto rocks and shells and wondered if that alone caused his injuries. He flailed his arms around on the gurney, yelled out, then passed out. It was a truly crazy way to conclude their night. Their fun turned to calamity. I hope they both lived to laugh about it.

Joe nudged me and looked toward the two guys with the duffle bag. Eddie was walking past them as he heard them say, "Fuck, missed them both." Joe insisted on retrieving their bag.

Eddie and the team followed them. "When we get up there by the crowd, I'll grab it, then pass it to the next guy."

Eddie made a spectacular fall onto the guy holding the bag and profusely apologized, offering to buy drinks for his clumsiness. When they rose, the bag had already traveled two blocks.

We met back at the house to go through the duffle bag. It held files of guests in the resort, complete with photos, combs in bags, used tissues in bags, financial information and even protected health information. The side pocket of the bag had a vial of liquid and several syringes. Was their intention to abduct these individuals for a ransom? What was the purpose of obtaining the health information?

Aunt Char woke up, looked at the table with everything laid out, and said, "Body snatchers." Rising, she went to bed.

We were clueless, but her idea seemed as reasonable as the rest.

Mickey turned his computer around to show the identities of the two men he captured in pictures for his databases. Criminals. Not terrorists. Joe made a call to his father, then the local police.

Two detectives arrived about an hour later and took the bag. We didn't mention capturing them on our cameras. The bag and their identity should incriminate them enough to prove their guilt in the resort thefts. Their intentions were suspicious, but it wasn't our role to determine if they were involved in organ theft, abduction, or extortion. Our work here was done.

Preparing to leave, I exclaimed, "What an easy day!"

They all recited in unison, "The only easy day was yesterday."

I gave them a questioning look, but they waved me off. We grabbed our bags and drove back to the hotel. Uncle Jim thanked us for helping him solve the mystery. I'm sure he'd boast about it throughout the resort.

DAY SIX

Déjà vu. Another day of waking up to Joe talking to his father on the phone. With a scowl, he paced and purposefully rubbed the back of his neck. "Send the files and we'll talk about it. I'm letting her make the call on this one. Bye."

He put the phone on the table and flopped into bed. I rolled over and said, "Tell me."

Joe gazed upwards, then turned his attention towards me. "It's New York. Your hometown specifically."

Now it was my turn to stare at the ceiling. I hadn't been back to Binghamton since the event that changed my life. Where my friends were murdered and I became a murderer. Flashes of it played like a movie on fast forward. My ears got hot, my breathing too fast and too loud. Fuck me. I threw off the covers and sprang out of bed. It was my turn to pace the room. Once the video started playing, it was hard to stop it. I needed to focus. Joe stood to count, soft and slow, but didn't approach me. He did what I should have done, trying to calm me. I got a grip after a couple minutes and told him he could stop counting. Sweat beads dripped from my scalp and down my chest.

"Has a group linked to the monsters reappeared?" I knew the answer. Is there any other reason to return?

He shook his head. "We don't have to go anywhere. And we aren't going back there." He grabbed his phone and said, "I'm calling my dad right now to pass on this one."

"Wait." What was I saying? "Just wait. Let me think about it."

He shook his head. "You don't have to. It's a terrible idea." He sat on the bed and watched me as I did just that.

"Can we review the files before I decide?"

He rubbed his face with both hands. "Joe, I see you're trying to let me decide, trying not to be my caveman and protect me. I appreciate that, I do. The perfect time to return there doesn't exist. It's not like we can perform an exorcism on my past. This is our job. So, let's go. And bring lots of weapons. Lots."

He half smiled and reached out for me. "We've got time before we respond. Let me show you how much of a caveman I can be."

Rocky called, saying he'd be at our door in five minutes to talk. We got dressed and waited for his knock.

He sheepishly entered our room and said, "I've got a favor to ask."

Joe didn't hesitate. "Shoot."

Rocky stammered, "Well, we're pretty close to Tampa and we have nothing pressing right now. Mind if I take a few days to visit our client, Ivy Grey?"

Joe said, "Ah, yes, our client Ivy Grey. Well, we have a new assignment in New York."

I jumped up from my chair. "I haven't agreed yet, but I need a few days to decide. I think you should follow up with the client to secure a five-star rating."

Both of them laughed, but for Rocky, it was an embarrassing one.

Joe proposed a week-long period to verify her security and staff competence. "We'll meet back at camp."

Rocky smiled his big perfectly fixed teeth grin, shook Joe's hand and gave me a big hug before he turned and left to go see his beautiful redheaded woman.

Ivy Grey and I kept in touch every few weeks after the fiasco that happened in Goldsboro. We've become friends and I've impressed upon her we'll continue to support her in any way we can. Apparently, Rocky has intentions of becoming more than friends. Since the moment he saw her, their chemistry was undeniable. Good for them, a love born out of chaos.

"Why don't we prolong our stay here instead of going back to camp? We can stay for the St. Patrick's Day party your uncle told us about." Joe stood with his hands on his hips, looking out the window. He didn't answer me, but took his phone out and called his dad.

"We'll be in New York next week. Start getting the details and package together for us. I'll send you the list of extra equipment I want for this one. If we don't have a drone up already, please get that in motion. I'll talk to you soon."

He sent a group text to everyone saying we were staying here until the 18th, then heading back to camp. Everyone had a free week. A few minutes later, everyone except Rocky was at our door asking questions.

"What? Nobody wants a vacation in Florida?" They looked skeptical until Joe added, "We have a job in New York next week. The trip is open-ended, and it's still cold up there. Let's enjoy some fun in the sun before going north." They looked unconvinced.

Eddie asked, "Where in NY?"

I answered, "My hometown."

Their eyes shifted from me to Joe until Bobby inquired, "Are you sure?"

Joe stepped forward and said, "It's an important mission that we'll deal with together. She's handled a lot on her own. She can handle this with us."

Alex said, "Ok, then. Let's head to the beach."

Bobby looked at me until I shook my head yes and said, "Yes, I've told you guys a hundred times. If I die doing this job, it's not your fault and I understand the risks. Just because I'm not military doesn't mean I'm not doing this for the same reasons you are. You wouldn't coddle a female service member, so don't do that to me. I mean, I want your support and all, but allow me to do the job."

Dusty, who usually stays in his own lane said, "As long as you stay present, you'll be a good asset."

I scoffed at him and grumbled, "You mean as long as I don't have a panic attack or melt down, I'll be valuable? Duh, Dusty."

He grabbed my shoulder and said, "Rachel, I'll go anywhere and do anything for you. Just make sure you're certain about doing this. Returning to a place of trauma requires a clear state of mind."

Bobby teased, "Well, look at you, talking about all the feels. And you're exactly right. Your deployments have made you aware of the importance of your state of mind."

Joe suggested, "Let's have a few days of fun before diving into this kind of conversation."

I supported Alex's suggestion to visit the beach and later the old folks' resort for tomorrow night's party planning.

Mickey sarcastically said, "Yeah, the rich old folks on vacation driving their million-dollar rides."

Rocky drove an SUV to Tampa, leaving us with our usual two vehicles for our trip to the beach. Uncle Jim told us to bring plenty of alcohol tomorrow and pick up some premade food from the local deli. They expected around fifty people to attend the private party at the resort.

There was plenty of open beach for us to choose our spot since it was only mid-March. It was mostly older couples and families with young children that were sprawled out on their blankets or low beach chairs. The towels and chairs we got still had price tags on them. Mickey and Eddie threw their stuff down, grabbed the new football, and ran to the water's edge to play. I watched them as they tried to find some single girls to throw it too close to. Men. The rest of us settled onto our towels and I had just closed my eyes when I heard a car alarm going off. Eddie and Mickey ditched the football and ran toward the parking lot.

Joe asked, "What's the chances it's ours?"

"We'll go check it out." Offered Alex as he and Bobby got up. Moments later, a whistle pierced the air, and we hurried towards the alarm.

The back of our SUV was open. A woman screamed as Eddie aimed his gun at a man holding a baby. Mickey held the woman as she pleaded with the man to release her baby. The guy holding the baby scanned the parking lot, searching for his backup or a way to escape. He yelled at them to stay back or he'd hurt the baby. We surrounded him as Bobby cleared the area, ensuring no one was in danger. The woman confirmed she'd never seen the man and that he broke the window of her car and grabbed the baby out of the baby's seat.

Joe inched closer to the knife wielding man, telling him to give him the baby. Behind us Dusty barked at someone, then we heard glass breaking and more yelling. Joe and Alex approached the guy from opposite sides, all the while Joe was talking to him for distraction. Alex charged him and punched him in the temple of his head, and Joe grabbed the baby. The guy swirled to the ground where he stayed.

Two police cars slid into the sandy parking lot as Eddie closed the back hatch of the SUV where all our weapons were. Dusty had yanked the driver of the getaway car through the window he just broke and walked him over to the police. The woman was still bawling as she held her baby and thanked everyone profusely for saving her. Joe, Alex, and Dusty stayed to give the police a report. The rest of us quickly departed, taking both vehicles to avoid any explanations about our weapons. We'd come back for the guys when they were done. Our beach day was a disappointment. Mickey reported that our arrival seems to have initiated a spike in crime in the area.

I shook my head and said, "Of course it did."

We drove back to the resort and parked at Uncle Jim's house. Their car was present, but they weren't home, so we walked to locate them.

Aunt Char was playing pickle ball again, and Uncle Jim was sitting outside the clubhouse drinking a Bloody Mary. We ordered some drinks and sat with him and two of his buddies. Joe texted, saying the police offered them a ride across the causeway and asked for our location. I told him and they arrived shortly after. Our early day drinking gradually transformed into an evening of bar-hopping, with more people joining us along the way.

Half the resort was at the bar and were indeed professional drinkers. Despite my intoxication, I stayed alert to defend against possible body snatchers. This fun, cozy town had a dark entity working here. Thanks to us, now four of the problems were off the street. How many more were there?

The older women loosened up, treating the team like their personal Chippendales. One woman put her hands on Joe's pec muscles and he politely backed up and walked over to me for protection.

I pulled him in close to me and said, "What's a matter, hot stuff? Can't fight them off by yourself?"

"Christ, these women are nuts. They act like teenagers on spring break trying to get laid while their husbands are too drunk to notice. I fear for my safety."

He feigned his fright, and we laughed as we spied Eddie getting his ass grabbed multiple times as he moved through the crowd toward the bathroom.

DAY SEVEN

My headache was so intense when I woke up, I thought I was already dead. My eyelids scrubbed like sandpaper on my eyes, my lips were dry and even my hair hurt. I heard the door shut softly and prayed it was Joe, because I knew that even a mouse had my number today.

Joe placed a glass of orange juice on the table and instructed me to sit up and finish it. Unpacking food, he asked if I preferred eating in bed or at the table.

I whispered, "Oh my God, Joe, I don't want to eat anywhere, or move, or breathe too hard."

He brought food over and told me, "Sit up and start eating. It'll help. Promise."

I pushed out from under the covers and nibbled on hash browns, a muffin, and another glass of orange juice. "I hope the old folks feel like this, too."

Joe said, "You can't keep up with us guys on drinking. Size matters, baby."

Joe texted, then announced, "We're leaving for camp today. No one wants to stay for the drunken shit show that St. Patrick's Day will be."

I appreciated it, as the idea of more alcohol made me sick. I lingered in the shower, then dressed and packed. My head hurt less if I moved like a sloth.

I collapsed in the back seat and slept the entire way back to base. I almost felt human when we arrived. The guys appeared to have recovered, as evidenced by their banter and eagerness to eat and drink upon our arrival. Size and experience do matter, especially when related to alcohol.

The bed called my name as I slunk upstairs and put my puny self to bed without dinner.

DAY EIGHT

Rocky was back from visiting Ivy Grey when we got up in the morning. I hated he had to cut his visit short. I pried into his business, but he didn't want to dish on any details.

I told him, "Never mind, I'll just ask her. She tells me everything." He actually gave me a dirty look. "What? Were you a jerk to her?"

Now he was insulted. "No, I wasn't a jerk. You needn't know everything."

I smiled and shrugged, took out my phone and pretended to text someone. He glared at me. His phone pinged with a text and he walked out of the room to check it.

From the other room he yelled, "Damn it, Rachel, that's not funny. How did you find that picture? So small, it's obscene."

I laughed and said, "It's called a baby gherkin. Get it? Little pickle?"

He threw a pillow at me, full force velocity, and knocked the coffee out of my hand.

"Holy Christ, Rocky, I didn't tell you, you have a little pickle. Even if you do, you possess many other endearing qualities."

The guys burst into laughter, and just as Rocky was about to show me his pickle, the General unexpectedly walked in.

General JD Cokely closed the door and took in the sight. Rocky stood frozen with his hands on his zipper. Coffee was all over the floor, pieces of my mug lay scattered at my feet, a pillow was on the counter, on top of my food where it landed, and Rocky's face was as red as his hair. The other guys got to their feet and gave JD an innocent look.

JD cocked his eyebrow, turned both his hands up and spread them sideways in a questioning way.

"Oh, JD, are you wondering what's going on? I can explain everything. Rocky went."

JD put his hand up to stop me. "Don't tell me." Rocky zipped his pants up and gave me another dirty look.

"Where's Joe?"

Eddie answered JD to say he was down at the range. JD nodded to me and left.

Rocky said, "For the record, it's like a zucchini."

We all laughed and dispersed to our rooms to get packed for New York. Mickey handed me a list of items I was responsible for gathering for myself and the team.

Joe returned after an hour and started packing and gathering his things. He remained mostly quiet until dinner. His silence fueled my nerves, but he didn't need my fear adding to his stress. Dressed for my workout, I ran into Eddie as I left for the box.

We sprinted to the box and partnered to complete all the challenges and finally the obstacle course. Eddie was well ahead of me today and made his fastest time. He lost weight and gained muscle over the last three months. Now he was six feet of pure strength and agility. Not killing Roger when he shot him has taken a toll on him. As a sniper, he was a perfectionist.

I plopped onto a bench and questioned whether I could make it back to the house by walking. He handed me a water and looked at this watch.

Three minutes later he said, "Get up, you get a twenty-second head start."

Fudge. I got up, threw my water at him, and ran for the house. He passed me halfway there, laughing.

I shouted, "Oh shut up, who cares if you're an elite trained military jerk picking on a small civilian woman."

He shouted back, "Poor loser."

Alex, Bobby and Joe were in the kitchen cooking.

Joe looked up and said, "Another freezer dump, lots to choose from tonight."

We ate in silence until I asked, "Can we talk about the elephant in the room?"

Rocky laughed and said we've talked about his giant part enough. Joe shot him a censorious glance because he wasn't there for the earlier conversation.

I laughed and said, "Seriously guys, I know you're all worried about me going back. I'll be fine, and if I'm not, I'll dial you in."

Bobby said, "Be sure you do."

Bed-time came early and Joe and I had our 'before going on a mission sex', which meant it was a long, serious, soulful connection that made me cry, quiver and fall into a deep, content sleep.

DAY NINE

The team packed three trucks with enough guns and ammo to start and finish a civil war. We divided and got into the vehicles, ready for the 12-hour trip to upstate New York.

We stopped for gas twice and filled up a couple of gas cans just in case. They said they'd come in handy if we didn't want to be seen getting gas.

We finally arrived at Chenango Valley State Park Cabins and had a special escort to get inside the park. We rented four cabins, easily in the off season. Shaded areas in the park still had patches of snow as we drove by. It was almost dark at 6:00.

Our escort provided us with all the keys, including the one for the hauling trailer between the two cabins. Stacks of wood sat outside each cabin, waiting to be used in weather like this. It's cold, gray, and not feeling very springy.

Joe walked over to the trailer and everyone followed to see what it held. Rocky extended his hand to halt him, swiftly scanning the surroundings for any potential danger. Dusty held his flashlight up to see the contents once it was open.

"Christ, what is all this stuff?" I asked. "That looks like a cannon."

Rocky's face lit up as he touched a weapon. "This will cause significant damage. No need for proximity."

Showing their excitement, they squeezed in to see what else was inside and purposefully grabbed a few weapons, as if shopping in a store. Joe handed me a couple of guns and a sack of something and we retreated to the cabins. Eddie pointed to one of the middle cabins and asked Joe if he was ok with it. I assumed it was so they could surround us for safety.

"Let's stow our gear and get supplies," Joe said. "Two people should stick around until we're set."

Mickey mentioned his intention to stay and set up his stuff while also placing some cameras outside. Alex volunteered to stay and help him. The rest of us loaded up and headed to two different grocery stores to get mostly boxed and ready to eat food, since the cabins weren't meant for gourmet cooking or even storing a lot of food.

I thought I recognized someone at the Price Chopper, so I put my head down and got really interested in reading the label of the protein bar I was holding. It was unlikely the girl I thought her to be would recognize me, seeing how different I looked. Damn if she didn't get closer to point out a better bar. She was staring at me, but I didn't even glance at her, though I knew it was Denice from high school. I thanked her and hurried away.

I found Joe and told him we had to leave asap. "Hurry up, we gotta go!"

He noticed my distress and b-lined it to the registers. He gave me the task of unloading the cart and instructed me to count and breathe while doing so. It helped me regain composure and exit the store calmly.

"What is it?" He asked when we got outside.

"A girl inside recognized me. I attended school with her. I know she knew me. What if she tells someone? Tells the wrong person?"

He gave me the keys and told me to get in the truck. I started it to get warm and waited for him to load the bags. I drove to the park, wondering if she recognized me and what her next move would be.

Joe said, "We'll get Mickey to check out her social media and do a background check on her."

Eddie called and said they were getting some fast food for dinner tonight.

Despite the cramped space in our cabin, we gathered together to eat and discuss the area. Mickey told us he and Alex put perimeter cameras up and alarms on each cabin, all linked to our phones. He then showed us three ex-military guys that were now in law enforcement that would be our backup and extra resources if needed.

Eddie said, "We've done everything we can for the day. I'm going to my cabin. Are you coming, dear?"

Bobby laughed and said, "Of course, darling." Rocky and Dusty, Mickey and Alex shared the other cabins.

Joe put a few more logs in the fireplace and we changed for bed, falling fast asleep in minutes

DAY TEN

It was freezing when we woke up. Joe slid out of bed and tended the fireplace while I stayed snug under the covers. As soon as it was warm enough in the cabin, we got ready and joined the team.

Mickey had three New York plates and inspection stickers to put on our vehicles, so we didn't stick out as tourists.

Today, we used two trucks to search for the whereabouts of these local terrorists. It seemed aimless to me, but Mickey was inputting the information from JD and cross-referencing all the details he thought would pinpoint their location or locations. We only had one to investigate today.

"I bet it's pretty around here in the summer." Eddie said.

I was the tour guide, telling them everything I remembered about Broome County. While trying to sound detached, I was fighting so many feelings, memories, and demons about my hometown.

I sat in the back seat with Mickey, who was skilled at multitasking - typing and talking simultaneously. He plopped his computer on my lap so I could see my former classmate Denice's entire history on his screen. He did an extensive search, not a social media search.

"Are there files like this on everyone?"

He said, "If someone like me is searching, yes. Nothing is private."

I was pleased to read her file and find out how successful she became.

In the lead vehicle, Alex stated their intention to drive up the hill for a drive-by near the suspected compound. Mickey grabbed his laptop back and pulled up a satellite image of the place. We pulled off the road and waited for their report.

Mickey said, "Make sure you are filming this and taking pictures."

"Yes, Mom." Joked Dusty.

Talking to his screen and typing, Mickey directed them to turn left and park at the house for sale. "You picked up a tail already. That didn't take long."

I said, "Jeez, what do they do, follow everybody that drives by their house?"

Alex was on the phone with us, while the rest crouched in their seats as the presumed terrorist's pickup decelerated to inspect their SUV.

Alex said, "I got my elbow on the windowsill, covering my face with the phone, and my hat is as low as I can pull it down. And I'm taking pictures. They better keep rolling."

Mickey advised. "They're turning around and heading back."

Joe urged, "Get out of there now. We can't risk a confrontation this early."

Alex squealed the tires and made it back down the hill without a tail.

"Looks like we'll be doing some hiking." Joe said. "We'll need extra vehicles to throw them off. We can't return there with that one."

"I wonder if they're always this paranoid or if they heard something?" I asked and immediately wondered if someone else recognized me from the store? Thoughts of me causing another catastrophe crept into my head.

Mickey said, "No chatter about you on here if that's what you're thinking."

My sigh told him it was.

Joe called his dad and told him we needed another team up here. His brother Jeff hadn't been back as leader of our second team since my Uncle Roger almost killed him before Christmas, three months ago.

I rubbed the raised skin on my stomach where he shot me. I hadn't decided on the design of a tattoo to cover more scars. I had hoped I was done with that, but I wonder if I'll ever be done with trying to make something ugly, beautiful. That emotion runs so deep.

We drove back to the park and stopped for Mickey to install a camera at the gate and several other places along the route to our cabins. Upon returning to the cabin, Joe proposed a hike and night in the woods. Everyone raised their hand except me. I looked around and raised mine, too.

"Oh, I guess that sounds like a lot of fun. Not."

Bobby said, "That's the spirit."

We studied the hillside and surrounding area of the compound from the satellite pictures to determine how we could get closer and put some devices out to actually hear them.

Rocky said, "We can use our new toys to check for their surveillance items. The metal detectors that pick up any kind of metal from 20ft away. These would have been useful over there."

Dusty agreed as he touched the scars on the back of his head.

"Ok, we can park our vehicles at the old abandoned school and walk up from there." Joe asked me if I had any information about it.

"It's been closed since 2002. I think it has asbestos inside. And they tell stories about the old teacher they named it after. I know little else about it."

Joe didn't seem to care about my answer and said, "For tonight, Rocky, Dusty and Bobby and I will go. We'll conduct a perimeter check and monitor the traffic on the hill."

Mickey said, "I've got some cameras for you, so maybe we'll catch some plate numbers."

They dispersed to change clothes and came back to our cabin in 15 minutes. Joe pulled me into the bathroom for a longer than normal goodbye kiss.

I pulled back and said, "You need to stop worrying about me and focus on your job. I'm fine."

He lifted my chin up. "I'm the first to know if you're not fine."

He opened our door and told the guys to load up.

That left Mickey, Eddie and Alex with me.

Eddie said, "Let's get some equipment and go for a walk."

By equipment, he meant weapons. I changed into heavier clothes and waterproof boots. It was still damn cold in March up here, especially in the sunless woods.

Rifles on our back, knives and handguns were standard, then we added night vision goggles, body cameras, the new metal detector, and hand-held heat sensors. I weighed at least ten pounds more with this gear. Mickey, the eyes for Joe and the group, stayed at the cabin. Alex walked into the woods first and said to keep ten feet between us. He scanned side to side with his detector. I was willy-nilly with mine and Eddie scanned vertically.

Their quietness was such that, if not seen, their presence would go unnoticed. As for me, the softer I tried to walk, the more sticks I crunched and leaves I kicked. We walked all the way to the lake when my sensor started flashing. I searched the trees but saw nothing. Eddie came to my side and moved his scanner around. Alex scanned his way back to us with his sensor flashing, too.

Eddie pointed to a tree, indicating a fishing line and a lure hanging from a limb. I laughed at the dreadful cast to get stuck way up there. We continued our hike around the perimeter of the lake and headed back to the cabin at dusk. My legs burned from the weight and the uphill trek back to the cabin.

Mickey was relaying information when we walked in and typing fast. Well, he always typed fast, but sometimes his intent was more evident. I was relieved to get rid of my metal weights and sit by the fire. These summer cabins were struggling to keep up with winter weather. You could almost feel a breeze coming through the doors and windows.

Eddie and Alex didn't disarm themselves while they searched for snacks, because they said it felt normal to have the weight of the weapons on them. Spending time outside in the cold always triggered my hunger, and now I was starving. I wanted warm, comfort food.

"Is it rude to leave for food while the guys are in the woods?"

Eddie replied with a mouthful of chips, "No. What are you thinking?"

"There's a couple of places right in Port Crane we could order from."

Alex agreed, "Let's go."

We chose from the menus and ordered before leaving. It took longer to leave the park than to drive to the restaurant. Alex got the food while Eddie and I sat in the parking lot waiting for him, watching the people inside. This place wasn't here when I lived here, but my screwed-up head saw my dead husband and friends inside, having fun. Completely different from when I last saw them. I covered my face with my hands and tried to calm down.

"Eddie, do you imagine things that aren't real? Like memories, but not genuine memories? Just really fucked up images?"

He answered, "Like your friends sitting around having a drink after they've had their arms and legs blown off, like it's possible to hold a beer like that? You mean shit like that? Yeah."

I felt better knowing I wasn't the only one, but worse, knowing Eddie had those images. He was the biggest joker in our team, and maybe the best actor.

Alex jumped in the truck and roared, "Roll. Now. Rachel, get down." Eddie had it in reverse before Alex shut his door and I slid to the floor in the backseat.

Eddie asked, "What the hell is it?"

Alex blurted, "I'm not sure. A feeling."

Eddie prodded, "A feeling? What feeling?"

Alex said, "Like an ominous one, Like the way this guy walked. Like."

I shouted, "Like who? My Uncle?" I've been carrying that sense since we got to Binghamton. They never found his body, and I knew that eventually he would find me. He didn't answer. "Alex!"

He turned and replied, "Maybe, I don't know." He contacted Mickey. "Get your eyes on this place. I need to see anyone who leaves."

I could hear Mickey's voice, then Alex said, "I don't give a fuck what you're doing, do what I'm telling you right now. Make it happen."

We chose a longer route to the park in case we were being followed. I think New York had us all spooked.

Alex apologized to Mickey as we walked through the door. Mickey didn't even shift his gaze from his screen, he just waved at him. I heated his food up and placed it near him, and peered over his shoulder to see what he was watching. He had nine boxes open with flashing images on two of them. He didn't like people hovering over him and gently pushed me away.

I scarfed my food down. I was nervous and scared. What if he was here? How many battles can we fight?

"Mickey, did you see the guy Alex was talking about? What's taking so long?"

He shot me a dirty look. Uncle Roger almost killed him, too. I got up and put my arms around him and squeezed for a second. "I'm sorry."

"It's not him." Exclaimed Mickey. "He's too short and his facial structure doesn't match. He's not a match."

His shoulders dropped an inch with relief, as did ours.

Alex said, "Sorry, guess I just got spooked. Something about him caught my attention."

"And what are you doing on that hill?" Mickey was talking to himself.

Eddie said, "Enlighten us."

"According to his tag and sticker on his car, and a quick search, this guy works for the mayor. What's he doing at 21:00, driving up the hill, going to the suspect's camp without challenge?"

The three of us hovered over Mickey's shoulders to watch what was happening. He was telling Joe, Rocky, Dusty, and Bobby who was coming their way. I noticed a person on the screen by the main house and inquired about them. Mickey said it was Bobby about to plant a camera and listening device.

Mickey shouted, "Don't move."

The mayor's aide pulled in and set off the motion detector lights in front of the house that lit up the entire perimeter. Luckily, Bobby was near the fuel oil tank and stuffed himself under it as much as he could. And it was actually the perfect spot to put the devices. I couldn't watch anymore. The suspense of watching him was killing me.

I heard Bobby's voice say, "It's a go. Waiting on your call to retreat."

Mickey said, "Copy that, hang tight." An eternity elapsed by before Mickey said, "All clear, move now."

The mayor's aide and two guys walked outside behind the house and started walking toward the oil tank. How lucky could we get as we picked their voices up on the device?

"I can get her to that location. I promise. The State Office Building is a regular destination for us. I can do it."

We looked at each other. "Is that thing supersonic or what?" I asked.

The two guys didn't seem to have a lot of confidence in him. "If you mess this up, everyone you know will suffer. You got it? It's a one-shot deal."

The aide said, "I can do it."

We watched him run back to his car and leave down the hill, then we all left Mickey at his computer. We finished eating. Sometimes I eat so fast I don't even taste the food. Maybe my nerves negate my taste buds because I only ever really enjoy eating when my mother-in-law, Betty, cooks for me.

Mickey mentioned that they have scheduled a ceremony to honor a murdered judge at the State Office Building in two days, at noon. "Why are they doing it there, I wonder, instead of the courthouse?"

I said, "We just call it the SOB for short."

Mickey pivoted his computer, revealing the courthouse and the SOB, so we didn't have to hover over him.

"Both the fire station and the police station are situated right there. If they have something substantial, it would obliterate everything."

He swung his computer back around and typed, then swung it back with a picture of the courthouse and an article about renovations on the steps and front entrance that started three weeks ago.

He said, "Guess that answers that question."

Mickey then relayed that information to Joe and said he would call the General. I asked Mickey if I could call, since I hadn't talked to mother-in-law, Betty in weeks, and I could just tell JD when I finished talking to her.

He looked at me sideways and said no. "Rachel, we don't just call the General, we have a special line. Any sensitive information goes through that number."

"I see Joe call him all the time. He said nothing about a special line. I call Betty and get through to her. Is it a secret? What number is it?" I whipped out my phone and looked up JD's number. "Ok, give me the secret number."

I felt slighted and clueless.

Mickey grabbed my phone and scrolled my contacts. "It's already in your phone, Miss sassy pants."

I checked the contact he pulled up. General Tso Take out.

"Are you kidding me? I've never seen this. Who put it in here? No one informed me, so how was I supposed to know? Totally useless. You guys suck sometimes."

I hate feeling stupid. I retreated to the bedroom and slammed myself on the bed.

Dammit. As soon as I got comfortable, I heard Mickey telling Joe three vehicles were coming up the hill. I rushed to the door, making the floor creak like Bigfoot's arrival.

Eddie snorted, "Oh, Rae, just come out here."

We stood behind Mickey and watched all the cameras and heat figures on the screens. He was identifying license plates and relaying everything he discovered over comms. The three trucks held two guys each, the house held five guys. All of them gathered outside by the trucks and stood near the truck beds. The listening device couldn't capture anything because of their distance, and we couldn't see inside the trucks either. They went inside the house and within minutes, emerged from the back door, lit a fire in the pit and stood around it, drinking beer. We could actually hear them talking when the fire crackles weren't too loud.

The snippets we heard from their conversation were frightening and included: level the block, leave town, they'll hear us now, dead judge. They sounded angry, and indifferent to the possibly hundreds of lives they were prepared to take. Unfortunately, they also sounded very well planned.

"We have just 48 hours to solve this?" I strained to hear more of what they were saying.

Alex assured me, "I'm sure this is being recorded. He can fix it so we can hear it better."

Mickey nodded. Then he hit a key and we could all hear Joe.

He said, "I think it's best to end this now. Explode whatever is in those trucks where they sit and hope it's not toxic. Waiting until everything is in place downtown carries too much risk. Too many unknown factors are potential for disaster."

Eddie said, "Ok, we're coming at ya."

He and Alex left our cabin to get their gear, and I got my heavier clothes and weapons together. I grabbed the ear communications, and we left in our newly delivered pickup.

Eddie drove the hilly, windy rode through Chenango Forks like an expert.

Mickey said, "Heads up, they're headed to their trucks."

Eddie said, "We're passing the old school now."

A second later, we heard a series of explosions. Eddie floored it.

Alex said, "Move your asses. That's going to generate a lot of traffic on this road."

Another tremendous boom shook us as we waited for the guys at the bottom of the hill.

Eddie and Alex both said, "Fuel tank."

The back doors opened and Joe and Bobby jumped in. Rocky and Dusty jumped into the pickup bed. Joe opened the rear slider to the bed and asked if they were okay. We drove them back to the school to get their vehicle, then drove the speed limit back to the park.

Joe said, "I think we took care of that problem."

Mickey confirmed it. "Oh, you definitely did. There's nothing on my screen except for fire. Four fire departments have been called in already."

Rocky said, "Can't wait to see the pictures."

I smiled. These guys were fearless and experts, and Rocky wanted to analyze them.

Everyone piled into our cabin upon returning and noticed the empty takeout containers. They talked shit to each other, then devoured half the groceries in the cabin over the next hour as we listened to the emergency channels, news broadcasts, and observed satellite images of the fire still burning.

Joe called his father, and it reminded me I was mad.

Accusingly, I asked, "Are you calling for takeout?" He eyeballed me funny and Mickey told him why.

He shrugged his shoulders and gave his father an update and then told us, "My dad spoke to the mayor and informed her about her aide. We will see her tomorrow as she wants to pursue an investigation into the attack's extent. Well, specifically Rachel is. We need to be discreet so the aide doesn't get spooked, although tonight should have him scared to death."

Dusty said, "Rachel is pretty scary sometimes. You sure you want to send her?" I slapped him on the shoulder before heading to bed.

DAY ELEVEN

"What should I wear? Do I have an appointment with her? What's my purpose?"

Joe rolled over and asked, "What's got you all fired up?"

Pulling the pillow from under his head, I questioned, "How did General Tso's number end up in my phone without my knowledge?"

He grabbed the pillow back and pulled me into bed. He was smiling as he rolled on top of me.

"I put it in your phone, and you handed it to me. I told you what it was."

"No, you didn't." He kissed my neck.

"Yes, Rae, I did. You were probably watching TV and ignoring me." He kept kissing me until I believed him.

When I arrived at the mayor's office for a 10:00am appointment, a receptionist, not her aide, greeted me. She was very feminine and professional in a skirt and blazer and I had on black from head to toe, including my wool pea coat. Mickey had already placed cameras and listening devices in the offices and stairways, anticipating the aide sneaking out to call someone.

Michelle Devine got up from her desk when I walked in, shook my hand and invited me to sit on the couch with her.

"Thank you for coming today. I hear we've got a rat in the hen house we need to eliminate." She was very direct. "I don't mince words, and I'm not inclined to die at the hands of a lunatic terrorist. So. Please help me avoid that and hopefully we can get concrete, prosecutable evidence on him for this conspiracy, before he gets to me. I'm told that the explosion last night would have devastated this entire city."

I agreed. "It took until this morning to control the massive explosion."

"Let me ask you a few questions. Do you own a firearm or have you ever shot a gun?"

She proudly said yes to both. "I was in the Airforce, and I remember my training."

"Ok, thanks for your service. And good. Do you have it with you?"

She got up, retrieved her purse and pulled out a lady Smith and Wesson revolver. "And before you ask, I have a daughter that I love and want to go home to, so if it's me or them, I won't hesitate to shoot them. I'm comfortable with this weapon."

I already liked her. "Let's discuss alternatives. You use whatever you can grab and to have a plan for each part of this room in case you're caught by surprise."

She clapped her hands together and said, "I'm ready."

"Let's look around the room. You've got a few heavy objects you could use for weapons. Your desk has a few sharps. The lamps, of course." I walked around and thought of scenarios. "What is this door?"

Michelle opened the door and said, "It's my get ready room, a bathroom and makeup area. I can lock it."

"Escaping your attacker is top priority. If you're unable to leave the office, go into that room. Lock the door and don't stand in front of it." I assessed the standard lock and recommended additional security measures. Then I pointed to her aerosol products. "In case they enter, these will give you some time. Spray them in the face. Throw everything you can pick up at them. Then get out the door. And if you can, get to your gun, otherwise, just run."

She nodded and followed along.

We walked out, and I stood by the office windows overlooking the arena.

She volunteered, "They aren't bulletproof and they don't open."

I looked down. "It's too far to jump, even if they opened. I guess you could shoot them out to signal for help. I'm sure they're thick, but they're breakable. An option if you're trapped."

She nodded, and we walked to the front of her office.

"Do you personally greet your guests, or does the receptionist handle that?"

"Usually she does, or she announces them and they let themselves in."

Two oversized wooden doors were between her and the lobby. Heavy curtains surrounded them, even without windows. I pulled the curtains back to see a plain wall. She mentioned the former glass wall, which she replaced with a solid one, but kept the curtains for aesthetics.

"That's convenient, as they're perfect for concealing weapons, such as knives. You can stitch a pocket in them or just use Velcro to secure your weapon of choice."

She tilted her head and said, "I see."

I kept walking around her office. It was spacious, almost 1000 square feet, I guessed. "Let me give you some quick thoughts- you can throw books, any furniture you can pick up, you can slice someone with a piece of paper, your letter opener, and your high heels are excellent weapons. If they get hold of you, go limp. Be dead weight and stop fighting. Aim for their eyes and gouge fiercely if you can reach. Or punch them in the throat. If they are standing over you, kick up between their legs. Kick an appendage in a non-standard direction, such as sideways towards the knee. Do whatever it takes to remain in this building. If they kill you here, it'll be a lot quicker than if they take you somewhere."

She walked around her office as if exploring it for the first time. She'd grab something and question the optimal body part for throwing it. Then she'd gauge the weight of it and act out the motions of using it. "I feel better already. You're a good at breaking it down."

Mickey was in my ear telling me the aide was entering the building, which I relayed to the mayor. I moved my gun to my coat pocket and unbuttoned it in case I needed the other treats I had on my body.

"What's the plan now? Are you going to stay and meet him?"

"Yes, I'm interviewing to be your new stylist. Crazy, right? Dressed like this, but it's so crazy he'll buy it."

He knocked twice and let himself in. He stopped in his tracks and his eyebrows shot up when he saw me. "I wasn't aware you had an appointment this morning."

He gave me a disapproving sneer and bluntly questioned my purpose for being here.

The mayor scowled and said, "Perry, I scheduled her myself. Now what can I do for you? And it's 11:00, where have you been?" She sniffed and got closer to him. "And why do you smell like gasoline?"

Mickey said in my ear, "Busted." He bit his nails and backed away from her. What a putz. I wondered how he had the nerve to get involved with the terrorists. He was wilting already, just being questioned by the mayor.

He finally stiffened up and said, "We have an appointment at 3:00 today. Off site, I'll send you the details." He hurriedly backed out of the office.

Mickey said, "No worries, I've got ears in his office."

I told the mayor, "Obviously, you're not going anywhere with him." I pointed to the couch, and we sat down. "Let's do car scenarios. You ride in the back?" She nodded yes. "Ok, if someone tried to drag you out, you try to pull them in. If they grab your legs, try to wrap your legs around them and starting beating their heads, scratching, whatever. Pull and twist their ears, put your fingers up their nose and pull as hard as you can. Punch them right under their nose and try to use your knuckles for that. But the rest, if all else fails, at least you'll have their DNA on you to identify them."

She asked, "You mean if they kill me and leave me somewhere, you can identify my killers?"

"Uh, yes."

She ran her hands up her arms and shook her head. "Perry must be into something pretty bad if he's still coming for me today. How many others are still out there? It's quite alarming they got another plan in place so quickly, don't you think?"

I agreed. "That's our motivation. Why we're FETCH. To teach you to defend yourself and to stop these groups."

She stood at the windows and said, "But there's always a chance they succeed and you can't teach someone or help them in time. Then what? Their group gets bigger and stronger for the next time they attack?"

I knew where she was coming from. "Number one, when you don't feel like a victim, you're more likely to succeed. You aren't helpless. We've shown others who had less to work with than you and they are thriving with confidence. There will always be a next time. Just focus on this time. What happens today? How do you come out the victor?"

Two knocks and Perry slithered in. "I'd like to leave around 2 for our meeting. I actually need to stop back at my house before our meeting."

The mayor stood and asked who they were meeting.

"A donor wants to meet at a building site to discuss his project plan with you to see if you'll be on board with him before he shows support for you."

It was hard to understand him because he kept touching his face in between words.

Her eyes were boring a hole through him. "What builder is it?"

He was backing up as he answered, "You've never met him. He wanted to be discreet, so I told your driver I'd drive us."

She nonchalantly waved her hand to dismiss him. "Whatever you worked out, Perry."

She could tell my opinion about him from my expression. She offered, "Civil service jobs are hard to be fired from. I try to pull the best out in everyone, but obviously something has gone terribly wrong with Perry."

I asked Mickey, "What's the plan? She isn't going, is she?"

He replied, "Ask the mayor if they always take the same car?"

She said, "Yes, always number 201. That's my assigned car." Mickey said, "I'll get back to you."

The next knock on the door was the receptionist delivering a big box. My first thought was a bomb. I was ready to shoot the windows to escape, but Mickey assured me it was safe. We opened it and found a bullet-proof vest, a comm for her ear, a holster for her ankle and one for her waist, and a container of pepper spray.

"They got that set up fast." I wasn't comfortable with this.

I walked away from her to ask Mickey, "Are you sending this untrained woman into an unknown situation with weapons she might not be able to use?"

He replied, "She won't be alone. As someone who has served in the Airforce and possesses a CWP permit, she has undergone training. We'll provide guidance. We can do this. Rae, we have bigger things to deal with." He was very matter of fact.

The mayor was trying to strap on the leg holster on her left ankle. "Are you left-handed?" She lifted her right hand. "Then put it on your right leg. Your wide pants allow easy access. Reach down your leg to retrieve it while seated."

She said, "Oh, yes, of course, I knew that, just got ahead of myself. Sorry." She glanced at me and said, "It'll be fine."

I knew they were working this entire plan out and the mayor would be safe, but it still made my stomach roll. She was holding up the vest and looking at her cream-colored silky blouse. "Do you keep any other clothes here?" I asked.

She strode to the door and asked the receptionist if they had dropped her dry cleaning off today. The woman rose and brought her an arm full of clothing in plastic. "Very good, thanks."

She handed me the clothes and asked me to pick a shirt for her. "Oh, you have a wool turtleneck in here, appropriate for a meeting outside. Here you go."

We walked into the dressing room and I helped her don the vest under the turtleneck. I noticed her hands were a little shaky when she was rolling her collar down. "Michelle, it's normal to be nervous. We will be as close to you as possible. Mickey will be in your ear to guide you and listen to everything. Casualties occurred in the fire last night, but apparently not the guy in charge, since they're still coming for you today. Hopefully, this meeting will net him and stop this local terror cell."

She inhaled deeply and asked, "Have you been working with the local police or state police on this?"

I shook my head no. "We play it as close to the vest as possible and only involve them when absolutely necessary. It's impossible to know who's involved or corrupted."

She said, "I see. So how many are on your team? I really don't have that much background on you, and I'm entrusting you with my life."

I wondered when she'd ask. "We are a group of eight in town. The guys are all elite military men. I became a hostage in a deadly home invasion in Binghamton over two years ago, but I survived and can share my story. My name was Rachel Smith. You might remember the incident?"

With her hand over her mouth, she sincerely apologized for not making the connection. "I wasn't the mayor then, but I remember the story in the paper. Of course, I never saw the details, only that you survived. How many died? Ten?"

I corrected her. "There were four terrorists and eight of us. 11." I turned and walked out into her office.

"Rachel, we still have at least an hour before I go. Can we continue our training? I feel different with the vest and guns on. Maybe I need to practice moving? It's been in a while since I was in uniform carrying a weapon. I keep my gun in my purse."

Perry entered without knocking, followed by a man in a suit. Michelle pointed her finger to scold him for barging in, but the man interrupted.

"Miss Mayor, I couldn't wait to speak with you. I hope you'll accompany me to our meeting, so we have the extra time to discuss my plans for this city."

Oh shit. I stepped forward and said, "Miss Devine, I have limited and highly sought-after time, and frankly, we've been interrupted enough today. You've paid for another hour of my time, which is non-refundable if you leave." I couldn't let her leave with them, even though it was the plan.

The man reached into his jacket and pulled out a money clip. He was peeling off bills as he approached me with a nasty sneer on his face. He showed me the money, stuffed it in my pocket and leaned forward to whisper in my ear, "Forget you were ever here, and beat it."

"Leave now," Mickey urgently instructed, "But first, make sure she has the communication device."

I stammered and tried to act nervous and said, "Mam, Miss Mayor, we can reschedule. If you'll just help me with this box, we can store it here for next time."

I grabbed the box and walked into the dressing room. She followed me and I shoved the comm in her ear and she loudly told me what a pleasure it was to meet me. Mickey heard her, and I gave her a thumb up motion. She peeked out, promising to join them once she finished in the restroom. Ignoring the man, I quickly left her office with my head down. I prayed she'd make it through whatever this day held.

I loitered at the receptionist desk on the pretense of making another appointment while trying to eavesdrop.

Perry poked his head out and suggested calling back tomorrow. "The girl left sick."

I smiled and said, "Oh, ok, thanks. Have a great day." I turned and walked down the hall. I got my phone out and called Joe. "Hey, girl, can you move up my next appointment? I'm done here." The hall appeared much more crowded than when I arrived. "I'm sorry, there's a lot of people here. Can you repeat that?"

Joe said, "Take the north exit."

I stopped him right there. "Girl, you need to explain that better. You know how I am with directions. Which exit is that closest to?" I was trying to sound like a clueless girl talking to her secretary in case this crowd was unfriendly. What the hell was he thinking giving me a direction like north?

He rephrased, "The arena is on your left. Keep going. That's north and take the stairs. You'll come out outside and I'll pick you up."

Jeez, was that so hard? "Ok, dear, thanks for being my travel agent today." I smiled at a man as I walked past him. He smelled funny but had a suit on.

I flew down the stairs and ran to the car. "Joe, something's happening, and it's happening inside her office. There were several unkempt men in suits that looked rough and smelled funny."

He squeezed my hand and kissed my cheek before asking, "Smelled funny how?"

Rocky cut in and said, "Describe the smell, Rae."

I said, "They stunk like they ate a garlic clove, except more chemically smelling."

After sniffing me, Joe commanded, "Get out of the car." He came to my side, pulled me out, unbuttoned my coat, threw it back in the car and slammed the door.

"What the hell?" I asked, and Joe and Rocky both said mustard gas. I said, "No, garlic."

Bobby and Dusty arrived, and we hopped in their car to head around the corner to the fire station.

Bobby ran inside and then called me in. "Take a shower and use this to cleanse yourself. Hot as you stand it."

Joe stood guard, instructing me as if I had never showered. He had my clothes in a red bag and a fireman's uniform for me to wear.

He explained, "Mustard gas was used a long time ago, a chemical that causes nasty blisters, burns, respiratory issues, and it somehow affects your blood cells, so it has some lasting effects, but it's usually not fatal. Usually. Did you touch anything in there? Did you touch the money he gave you? You smelled like you did."

I said, "No, I'm telling you they all smelled. The hallway stunk, and I walked through it. Like walking through one of Eddie's gas attacks, it must have got on me."

They all keyed in and echoed, "Copy that."

We walked into the Fire Chief's office to explain the situation to him. He listened and asked if we informed the Police Chief, and who exactly we worked for. He was skeptical and didn't uncross his arms as he eyed us. The mayor was in real danger and he was thinking about protocols.

I put my hands on his desk and said, "Sir, I'm Rachel Smith, the lone survivor of that home invasion that happened here a couple of years ago. Terrorists have returned, plotting to destroy this building, the neighboring one, or even the entire city. We blew up their bombs last night, but they must have chemical weapons, too."

It finally sunk in as he reached for the phone and yelled for one of his guys to come into the office. The old man transformed into a seasoned professional in one second. Impressive.

The fire department, dressed in hazmat suits, lined up, waiting for orders. Moments later, the fully geared swat team burst through a door and requested a sitrep. Joe introduced himself and gave a concise report and detailed mission.

They immediately ordered a shutdown on all the power, HVAC equipment, and disabled the emergency power for the entire downtown area. The police were evacuating people in the area, starting several blocks away. The city was on lockdown and they'd placed barriers around the block. These crazy terrorists had the mayor trapped inside with them. And for what? I hope Miss Devine can survive this.

Mickey had positioned himself across the street at the arena on the outside walkway. He was about even with her office windows.

Joe said, "I'd like for you to go over with Mickey. Please. You can help from over there."

Despite wanting to protest, I recognized their stress. Thus, I complied with the leader's request and hurried across the street to stand with Mickey.

It was a struggle to climb the stairs with my ill-fitting uniform and shoes. I was huffing when I reached Mickey. "What's going on with the mayor? What are they saying?"

He sarcastically said, "You been smoking?" Then said, "Wait, do you feel ok? Did the gas get you?"

I bent down to roll up my pants and glanced up at Mickey to respond when I saw the red dot on his chest. I grabbed him and pulled him below the cement wall while screaming what I was doing. Mickey informed the others and Joe responded it was the SWAT team and he told them of our existence.

"Well, jeez, thanks for that," I said. That about scared me to death.

Mickey asked, "Are we clear?"

Joe said, "Clear. We're sending a couple of guys over to you now."

We stood up again. He informed me that a man and Perry remained in the office with the mayor, but their evil plan remained undisclosed. From our vantage point, we saw people leaving the city on foot and in cars. They had barricaded the bridge to incoming traffic and diverted it around the city. Police moved swiftly to set a perimeter around the building and placed their men on rooftops. The terrorists probably see that too.

Mickey reported that the individual with the mayor was aware of the situation outside. "Expect some action."

Two SWAT guys came to set up near us and reported their positions.

Mickey advised the mayor to distance herself from the men. We must have distracted them enough them for her to run to her dressing room because she whispered, "I'm locked in my dressing room. I think they know you're out there."

Mickey advised her to block the door and stay clear of it because of fumes.

I asked, "How do you deliver the mustard gas? Is it in a bomb?"

The SWAT agent volunteered that "It doesn't take a bomb, they can disperse it in several ways, such as in the water, vapors, and they can immerse objects in it. The vapor is heavier than the air, so it doesn't rise, just settles in low places. Let's just hope that it was correctly identified and isn't mixed with anything else more toxic or fatal. It's hard to make large quantities of that stuff."

Oh boy, they were just going on my description of garlic, so what if I'm wrong?

"Breach in two minutes."

Mickey alerted the mayor of a breach in two minutes and advised her to remain still. She said they were trying to get in her door, but she locked herself inside the bathroom so she didn't know their progress.

I got closer to Mickey and yelled through his comms. "Don't hesitate. Shoot anyone who enters. Unload both guns into them."

"In 60." "30." "Go time."

We heard a flurry of gunfire, some tinny, some loud thudding noises, breaking glass, and then silence occurred in about a minute. I remained silent until we received the all clear and everyone, including the mayor, checked in.

Firemen in full gear arrived with hazmat trucks at the fire station across the street, preparing a decontamination area. A large crime scene truck pulled up with staff already geared up, covered head to toe.

I looked at Mickey and said, "We've had a helluva 24 hours, right?"

He was typing on his keyboard and barely looked at me, but gave me a distracted fist bump.

I hit my comm and advised, "I'm on my way across the street and going to find the mayor." I needed to see her with my own eyes.

A fireman approached me at the stairs, shook my hand, and said, "Nice work."

I said, "You, too." About ten steps down, I felt queasy and grabbed the railing, waiting for it to pass. I couldn't decide whether to turn back, sit down, or continue to the bottom. The fireman that I just spoke to was at my side, taking my arm, telling me he'd help me. Black circles floated in my eyes as my knees buckled. His gloved hand pulled the comm out of my ear. My jelly-like body was helpless to fight back or even scream out. Not this again.

DAY TWELVE

I woke, but didn't move, vacillating between the urge to scream or cry. A cold liquid entered my arm through an IV. Then I heard it. An announcement. I opened my eyes to see a dimly lit hospital room and Joe sitting in the corner. Holy Christ, what a sight.

"Joe." My throat was raw like I swallowed razors. "Joe?" He literally jumped out of his chair and sat next to me on the bed.

"Hey, Rachel." He picked up my hand and kissed it.

"What happened?"

He looked tortured as he rubbed my hand and said, "I failed you again. I'm sorry."

I rubbed my eyes and asked again. "Explain that, please. Was it Uncle Roger?"

He moved me over in the bed and maneuvered his massive body beside me. "No, Babe, it wasn't. He was local. He touched you with a sedative. Try to sleep some more."

I rolled on my side and curled into him. With his arms around me, I fell back to sleep.

When I woke back up, Eddie and Bobby were in my room eating Spiedie subs. Seeing I was awake, they placed one on the tray in front of me.

Eddie said, "You woke up just in time to prevent me from eating your sub. You were right, these are good."

They kept eating and looking at me. Bobby handed me the bed controls but said nothing. I raised the head of my bed to full sitting. The marinated chunks of chicken made my stomach growl for them. I opened up the sub and pulled a piece off and stuffed it in my mouth. I didn't talk until I finished the entire sub that originated and was only available here in Binghamton.

I wiped my mouth and asked, "What's new?"

Eddie answered, "They're still investigating all the people involved, 22 of them, so far, from the house and yesterday's event. Some are dead, of course, 31 civilians are in the hospital being treated symptomatically for the exposure, but they'll be alright."

I asked, "And the guy that drugged me?"

Bobby said, "A SWAT guy saw him trying to carry you away and neutralized him."

I drank my lukewarm water and pondered, "If that guy was outside dressed like a firefighter, there must be others. And they know about me. Are they part of the original group? How did they recognize me so quickly? My tats were covered until I got changed at the fire station."

Bobby told me to slow down. "You get yourself all wound up and start talking a million miles an hour."

He pulled out his phone and called Mickey. "Review the outgoing calls made by firefighters on duty yesterday, immediately after Rachel's arrival at the station."

"I'd like to leave now." They both heard it in my voice. The tone before I go into meltdown.

Bobby said, "Let me get someone in here to disconnect you, Ok?"

Eddie placed a bag of clothes on the bed and closed the curtain for me. I pulled the IV bag off the stand and fished it through the arm of my bra and shirt, then I got my underwear and pants on. I opened the curtain and asked for my shoes.

A doctor and nurse walked in with Bobby. I extended my arm to the nurse and requested her to remove the IV. She waited for permission from the doctor.

He said, "I'd really like you to stay another night."

I looked at him, then pulled the IV out of my arm.

"Can I get a Band-aid?"

The nurse promptly provided one and exited the room. The doctor said I was leaving against his orders.

I said, "Thanks for your help, but I have to go."

I finished putting my shoes on and we left. Bobby walked in front of me, Eddie next to me with his hand at my elbow. Within minutes of expressing my need to go, we were outside in the cold, fresh air.

"I was in this hospital after it happened. The thoughts just kept building and building. I had to get out. Thanks."

Bobby said, "We got ya, don't worry. The city buildings are being ventilated, so the investigative teams are meeting at the riverside hotel. We're going there now."

Eddie tugged my sleeve and said, "You're on notice. Don't go anywhere without one of us. Not to the bathroom. Not to scratch your butt. Not to pass gas. Nowhere."

I punched him in the arm and said, "I wish you'd go somewhere to pass gas instead of sharing it so freely with the rest of us."

He said, "Got no idea what you're talking about."

Joe stood by the hotel door as we arrived. He gave me a brief hug and whisked me inside.

He called the entire team over once inside and said, "Two on her, constantly. And keep your heads on swivels for anyone looking at her or trying to take pictures, or whatever. You know the drill."

FETCH shifted into high alert mode. They were lethal soldiers on the enemy's front in my hometown.

The agencies investigating had set up in the ballroom on the main floor. People in various uniforms and suits sat intermingled at the tables. Seeing me walk in, the mayor rushed over to hug me, leaving the man she had been speaking with in limbo.

In my ear, she said, "Spending that time with you before that happened saved my life. It happened so fast I didn't have time to be scared. Well, actually I was terrified, but I felt confident too. Thank you, and I'm so glad you're ok."

I said, "Thanks, and I'm glad you're ok too. Could've been a lot worse."

She looked at her phone and said, "The governor will be in town tonight. We're getting a lot of attention. There will be an abundance of cameras tonight, if you need to avoid them."

Joe nodded. "Yes, we certainly want to avoid that, thanks. Let's get back to work, okay?"

Joe escorted me to a table with four men and a woman that he called our station. Before I sat down, Eddie pulled me away and said we needed to restock. Joe nodded, and we ducked behind a partition so I could put my knives and guns away. More than I usually carried. I didn't ask, just tried to find spots to put them. Eddie just tilted his head and asked if I was set.

"All good." Even though I wasn't. I remained uneasy about the hospital and became increasingly paranoid about someone in the room wanting to kill me. He walked me back to Joe and sat next to me.

Eyes fixed on the keyboard, the woman revealed, "We've confirmed the caller's identity. He's just two tables away.

Let's not be like high school and have everyone stare, though." She glanced at me.

I said, "Oh hell, I'm going to look, and I'm going to get up and beat his ass. Who is it?"

She covered her grin with her hand and said, "Do you want some help or are you going lone ranger?"

Another man cleared his throat and said, "Let's use some discretion, maybe wait until he leaves the room, to, um, beat his ass." He peered over his glasses at me and smirked, then added, "He may be in cahoots with someone else in the room, so, I say again, be discrete."

I rolled my eyes at him. The woman disclosed the person's identity, Joe texted FETCH, and the rest reached out to their teams as well. We just needed to wait for him to exit the room.

An hour ticked by. "I'm going to pull the fire alarm." I made a joke, but the table's stern look implied Joe had to rein me in. "Hey, I'm just kidding." Glancing between Joe and Eddie, I asked, "Can we go for a walk or something? I need to move around some."

They both stood and Joe said. "I got it." We walked away from the table.

"You got it? Like I'm an it?" I didn't look at Joe and shrugged his hand off my elbow.

He firmly placed his hand on me once more, saying, "Not now, Rachel. The subject stood up as soon as we did. Stay alert."

We passed the double doors of the ballroom and turned left toward the main lobby. Dusty sat, holding a newspaper, on the left side. Alex stood on the right, on his phone.

Joe said, "As soon as he gets in the middle of you two, take him." With his gun out, Joe kept his left hand on me. He expected greater trouble than from one man. "Don't leave my side, don't get separated."

I glanced at him and said, "I won't."

Hearing the commotion, we turned around. Dusty had the man on the ground, sitting on him to secure his hands with zip ties already. He and Alex got him to his feet and took him by the arms to walk toward the lobby. They led him out of the building and we walked back into the ballroom like nothing happened.

The woman at our table mentioned that another woman followed us and stopped near the double doors. Upon seeing what happened, she returned to the room. "She's been texting since she sat down."

Joe asked about her connections. The man at our table threw his glasses on the table after reading a message on his phone. "For Christ's sake, she's got a 'community organizer' name tag on. Who vetted the people in this room?"

Bobby was squatting next to her the next time I glanced her way. He was smiling, but she was pale and fidgeting. He stood up as she handed him her phone, then he pulled out her chair and escorted her out of the room, nonchalantly passing her phone to Mickey on the way out.

How do people get brainwashed to believe bombing and killing convinces others? How do they so easily figure out my identity? I look completely different, changed my name several times and have moved around. It can't be just because I'm with FETCH now.

The woman Bobby removed from the room had a nice, albeit prissy, demeanor. How does she fit with this crazy scheme? And why do they all think it's ok to kill me? What is the endgame? Joe nudged me, gave me a stern look, and told me to pay attention. I was mad at everyone tonight, including Joe. I felt like I was adding to the problem here, not helping. Many people die when I'm around. Take no prisoners was the apparent motto.

Mayor Devine confidently approached the front of the room, causing everyone to turn their heads. There was a long table near the wall, positioned like a bridal table. Applause followed her steps, but she didn't waiver. She put her hand up to stop the clapping and began talking to make it end quicker.

"Thank you all for being here, trying to figure out this act of terrorism. But before we go further, my deepest thanks go to all the agencies, named and unnamed, for their quick response to saving the city and my life today. The battle to uncover all involved parties aiming to tear down our government has just begun. We'll only stop when the last person is apprehended." She provided an up-to-date report on the past 24 hours, but excluded most of our involvement. She declined questions and promptly returned to her work.

Mickey texted everyone saying that the woman's phone had sent a group text, with several numbers in New York City and Albany. Joe inquired about specifics, and Mickey assured him of a prompt update.

Local and State Police were here, guarding the mayor, making it hard to approach her without showing credentials. She was oblivious to her surroundings, engrossed in phone calls. Filtering in, one by one, were four men dressed in suits with hardware under their jackets. They were too unkempt and wore cheap shoes to be part of an elite team like the secret service. So, who were they?

Joe directed FETCH to the room's perimeter, and he and I went to the doors. Shadows fell upon the four suit-clad men in the way of Rocky, Bobby, Alex, and Eddie. Mickey was somewhere working on his computer and Dusty was approaching the mayor. Joe told me to keep scanning the room and watching Dusty's back. No one in the room noticed the commotion on the outside edge.

I informed everyone that the doors near the mayor lead to the outdoor patio next to the river. That was the nearest exit, but then you were trapped outside.

The mayor glanced up, searching for us at the table. Panic crossed her face when we were not there. She scanned the room and found us with the biggest question on her face. Dusty loomed before her, motioning her to the doors with the slightest movement of his head. One hand on her ear, the other clutching the phone, she acted like she couldn't hear and headed towards the doors.

The officers watched her, unaware that Dusty had already stepped onto the patio. She looked at Joe before she exited, and he nodded his head for her to go. The officers never moved, making me think they were fakes.

The four suits finally noticed the hulks next to them in black outfits and nervously searched their counterparts for direction. Joe instructed me to scan the room as the guys could handle themselves. Eddie and his goon were the closest. I heard a grunt, then a thud, as Eddie took him down. It happened similarly to the other three.

The fake police stood and watched, but didn't move. They were outnumbered. Despite some men in the audience attempting to intervene, the fakes opted not to. Joe and I distanced ourselves from the imposters at the front of the room. How could the local police be present without the real locals identifying the imposters? It's not that big of a department.

Properly suited men approached the four imposters at the front table, who tried to escape through the door Dusty had taken the mayor through. They were in cuffs before they made it out.

Nearly all 50 individuals in the room noticed the ruckus and attempted to depart. Most people gathered their documents, computers and briefcases while others left in a hurry. The law enforcement officers stood with hands on their holsters, unsure of whom to stop. A wave ebbed toward the exit.

Dusty came on comms and said he could use some help outside.

Joe grasped my hand, placing it on his belt, emphasizing for me to hold on tightly. He forcefully maneuvered through the crowd, leading us to the patio just in time to witness the mayor's scream and two loud splashes. Joe stopped me from running toward the river and pointed to two men walking along the river wall. We hurried along close to the building until we caught up with them about the time they were taking aim at our friends in the river. Joe swiftly eliminated the two men, leaving me no time to even consider pulling out my gun. He was so damn fast.

We ran out toward the river wall to look over the edge. We spotted Dusty and the mayor standing near the edge of the wall on some clogged debris. Joe leaned over and said send her up. Dusty squatted down and the mayor stood on his shoulders and scratched her way up the wall until Joe grabbed her hands and hauled her up. He then took his coat off and Dusty jumped up to grab it and walked up the wall as Joe pulled him.

"Christ, Dusty, you weigh as much as a VW bug." He looked at his stretched-out coat, shaking his head as he put it back on.

I asked, "Michelle, are you ok?" She shivered her response, "I just don't understand any of this."

Sirens shrieked from all directions as they converged on the hotel. Mickey informed us he got confirmation that the officers weren't actually officers and had got away, but they took the four men in suits into custody after Mickey got their fingerprints, just in case they ended up making a mysterious jail break.

The mayor, wrapped in a silver blanket, spoke to the Chief of police in the lobby. Mickey was standing behind them, innocently working on his computer. FETCH surrounded them and I looked over Mickey's shoulder at his computer. He was reading text messages and the phone logs of the man in front of him.

I asked, "How can you do that?"

He shushed me and said, "Do you not realize my magic talents yet?"

He gave a thumb up to Joe, who said Joe, "Let's take this conversation somewhere more private."

We entered a smaller conference room where Mickey and Alex checked the room for cameras and Dusty stood outside with the door left open. Mickey informed them that the woman that was listed as a community organizer texted two people in NYC that worked at that mayor's office and one person at the State Capital building in Albany.

"We don't know who they are yet, just their location."

The Chief questioned, "Is all this for some political bullshit? What are you involved in, causing all this trouble?"

Michelle flung her blanket off and stood to face him. Her face was beet red and her chest heaved, but she said nothing. Realizing his error, he tried to reword it, but she signaled for him to halt.

She inhaled and exhaled loudly before she said, "I have been working my ass off trying to get this city back on track after my predecessor almost ran it into a drug and crime ridden, poor house. I have been fighting policies that NYC sponsors, trying to make Binghamton a safe place to call home. That's what I'm involved in. Common sense politics without corruption."

The Chief apologized. "Michelle, I know you're honest. How is NYC involved in these events? And you specifically?"

Mickey was still looking at his computer when he asked, "Do either of you know Sam Hill, Mike Hill or Jenna Hill? They have a pretty low digital footprint, but some irregularities."

He glanced at the chief with an expectation of recognition. The chief paled and dragged a chair out to sit down. He realized his life was about to change.

"My brother-in-law and his two kids. What is their involvement?"

Joe stepped toward him and looked down at him. "Why don't you tell us, Chief?"

He glanced at Joe, then rested his elbows on the table, shielding his face with his hands.

"He was always, uh, eccentric, never holding a job for very long. His wife got cancer a few years ago. They didn't have insurance, not that it would have mattered for long with brain cancer, but she died and he blamed everybody, from the insurance companies to big pharma to the government. We haven't kept in touch too well with them after she died. It was my wife's sister." He glanced around and inquired about Sam's involvement in this. "He's not smart enough to plan any of it, and I haven't seen him around in the last 24 hours."

Mickey said, "Bingo. I guess the daughter hates the world for her mom dying. Look at this page I found. It's hers."

He turned his computer to show Michelle and Joe. The mayor looked angry and then sad.

Joe said, "She's the instigator. What's her connection to the guys in Chenango Forks?"

Mickey sat down and typed until he got the answer. "Surveillance cameras capture her car ascending the hill after the explosion. And her phone, wait, let's see, yep, text messages between her and several people up there."

I questioned the status of the dad and brother.

The chief answered, "She's the smartest of them, and she's pretty. Probably able to talk the crazies into doing her dirty work."

In a tired tone, the mayor questioned, "What's the purpose? What did they think they'd gain by blowing up downtown, poisoning people, and killing me? What payback does that get for her mother's death? And what's the connection to NYC politics?"

The chief asked, "Could it be unrelated and just an epic coincidence of events? The political players taking advantage of this chaos to add some fuel to their agenda?"

He was recovering from the shock of his in-law's involvement and tried to connect the dots away from them, at least partially.

Joe advised Mickey to send this information to the general if it has not already been done. "We need some more manpower to track down the folks in NYC and Albany. We'll require additional teams for backup, but not local ones."

The police chief said, "My department isn't corrupt." With a wave of his hand, he confessed his lack of knowledge about those involved. "Go ahead, bring in another agency to help. I need to get my wife out of town and ensure she avoids them, and vice versa." He hung his head and I could feel his embarrassment in his posture.

Bobby and Alex entered, announcing they secured hotel rooms for all of us. "They cleared out the top floor for us, including the mayor." Bobby looked at Joe for his approval.

Joe said, "That sounds like a good plan, Bobby. The mayor and Dusty need to change out of their soaked clothes. Can someone accompany them while we wrap up before calling it a night?"

Alex said they'd bring our gear in from the vehicles and check in with us shortly.

The chief stood as if to leave, and the mayor stood with him. "Chief, I don't need to stress to you the importance of keeping this quiet. I know you're in a tough spot, being relatives, but they can't know we know."

He pounded the table and declared, "I'm well aware of all of that. And that my wife lost her sister and is probably going to lose the rest of her family. Not noticing any of this is inexcusable. And there's not a damn way I keep my job. Might even lose my wife. I'm aware of all of it."

Joe stood between them and suggested, "You and your wife need to get out of town, not just her. Tell her you had threats against you and you have to leave."

The chief's face flushed as he said, "What am I? A damn pussy? I'm the chief of police, for God's sake. I can't turn tail and run. I won't."

The mayor said, "Shouldn't you recuse yourself from the case? Whether you want it to or not, your relationship with them will come out. Maybe as soon as tomorrow."

The chief threw his hand in the air and said, "I guess I'll go home and tell my wife we're going away for a few days." That was a man twisted with emotions.

Rocky had switched places with Dusty so he could go get changed earlier, so Rocky, Mickey, Joe, Michelle and I headed to the elevator and rode to the top floor. Upon the door opening,

Alex directed us right with a wave. "We're all on this side of the elevator, except for Dusty. He'll be in the room beside the stairs. Maybe Rachel and the mayor can room together tonight?"

I spoke up before Joe could. "That'll be fine. We'll be fine."

Alex and Joe checked the room. Again. My gear was already in here, so I know they thoroughly checked before it.

"Keep the blinds closed. Don't open the door to anyone but me."

I saluted Joe, gave him a kiss, and shooed them out.

"How about washing your clothes in the sink and then you shower? I'm sure they have laundry service here, but I'm guessing that's off limits for us tonight."

The mayor wrapped up in a towel and we worked together to wash her clothes and rig up a clothesline by connecting the hangers together over the chairs near the heating unit. As she showered, I hid my weapons and felt secure enough with her ability to use them.

I showed Michelle where I hid everything and gave her a quick how-to with the guns. The knives were self-explanatory. She was shocked that I had all those weapons on my body.

I took a long shower to rinse off the hospital smell. When I came out, Michelle was in her bed and said, "I'd love to pick your brain some more, but I'm so exhausted, Rachel, that I just have to sleep."

I turned my light out and said, "Mayor, you had a helluva day. We can talk in the morning."

DAY THIRTEEN

Joe texted me at 5:00 am. "Are you awake?"

"I am now, dear. Can we get some coffee and breakfast? I'm starving. Big surprise."

He texted back quickly, "I'll deliver it in half an hour. Both of you get ready."

I put my feet on the floor and told Michelle to wake up. I startled her, but she flung the covers off like she'd been awake. "How did you sleep?"

She ran her fingers through her shoulder length hair that wasn't curly yesterday.

She saw the surprised expression on my face and laughed. "Oh, this? Yeah, without tons of product and a good blow dryer, I have this mess." She got up and limped over to her clothes.

"Why are you limping? What's wrong?"

She sat in the chair and inspected her right ankle.

I got up to inspect it and said, "Holy shit, that's a big ankle. When did that happen?"

She raised her leg up and rubbed her ankle. "I guess when we jumped in the river. Didn't even notice it last night."

"That's what adrenaline does," I said.

I texted Joe and asked him to bring ice for Michelle's ankle when he brought our breakfast. She limped to the bathroom to dress while I got ready in the room. Joe called to say he's outside, knocking on the door. To appear compliant, I stayed on the phone and checked the peephole. With a quick kiss on my cheek, he entered the room and set down the bags.

Alex knocked on the door and had ice and a wrap for her ankle. He attended to her while we ate and she talked on her phone to other state officials.

The corner of her eyes crinkled when Alex tightly wrapped her ankle. He looked up and said, "You'll thank me later."

She was still talking on the phone but mouthed a thank you and let him pick it up and lay her leg on pillows for elevation.

Ending the call, she conveyed her increased confusion because of the newly discovered puzzle pieces. "The Chief is cooperating fully and supplied some more insight to his brother-in-law. Investigations are being conducted on the murdered Judge and his cases. My assistant Perry is speaking to anyone who will listen. It seems his involvement was purely monetary to solve his gambling debts. He said he wasn't a trusted core member of the group, but that he was willing to sacrifice me for a clean slate financially."

I shook my head and said, "Wow, that's a lot to take in."

Joe gave his official update. "Background checks are presently being conducted on all employees in the city, with individuals stationed in NYC and Albany overseeing those implicated in those regions. They're going to pick up the chiefs' relatives today as soon as they're found. We'll return to the Chenango Forks hill to search for remaining clues. And we've got four men to guard you as you deal with things on your end. We've got a room set up for you downstairs to use."

We escorted her down the elevator to the designated room, where Joe gave specific orders to the men that would guard her. FETCH then started the trek up to the hill. Joe, Mickey, Eddie and I were in the first vehicle.

"Are we thinking this is two separate groups here? It seems like a pretty big operation to just be based on one man seeking revenge about his wife dying." I asked.

Eddie and Mickey both laughed. "What do you think your husband's potential is? You wouldn't be able to count the casualties. He'd burn the entire city down."

I said, "Well, she had brain cancer, whether she had insurance or not. And the local crowd isn't rich enough to pull this off. So that makes me think the original group I know is involved. And they know about me being here. But how did they come together to plan this?"

Mickey mentioned receiving the fire report. "The truck with the tank carried airplane fuel. Several other storage tanks on the property had old engine oil, kerosene and diesel. No toxins, they just wanted their target to burn long and hot."

Joe said, "They wanted to wreak havoc and by taking out the police and fire station, they'd get a lot accomplished in a short amount of time."

I pounded on the window. "These people are fucking psychos. What do they think they can accomplish? Government isn't perfect but what's their plan? A free for all? The wild west?"

Joe said, "Yes, they are psychos. And we need to stop them, all of them. Spectacularly eliminate leaders, leaving followers too scared to act. That's the plan." He looked at me in the rear-view window and said, "Plan it, work it, time it. Right?"

Joe saying my dad's motto gave me focus. And I really needed to have my shit together for what would happen next. I only wondered for a second when I became a shoot first and ask questions later kind of person, but that's who I am.

I took out all my weapons as we drove and double checked them as fully loaded and my knives sharp enough to slice through pretty much anything-animal or mineral.

We smelled the ashes before we got there. The cold air kept the fuel odor strong near the property. We pulled into the driveway and saw mounds of debris scattered for about half an acre. A couple of craters marked the spots where something had exploded, creating holes. The scene was black and white, depending on what and how it burned.

Rocky was out of his vehicle and walking around before anyone else. We sat and watched him for a few minutes, stopping to look at something, picking things up and smelling them, moving to the next object that caught his eye. While kicking ashes, he took pictures in search of the unknown.

Eddie and Mickey got out, leaving me and my husband. Joe turned around, resting his hand on the passenger seat. "Rae, I won't sugarcoat this, because you don't need that, but this group obviously knows about you, and, yes, I think it's some faction of the same group that Michael embezzled from. So, trust no one. Shoot to kill if confronted, don't hesitate, stay focused and always stay with one of us. No matter what, never get separated." Then he reached back and squeezed my knee. "Never forget that you're a born and bred badass, and the absolute love of my life. I want you every day, for eternity. Stay vigilant."

After the pep talk, he exited and waited for me to accompany him around the property.

The temperature was in the 20s; the sky was overcast and the wind swirled in circles. A yucky day in March to traipse around a burned-up hillside. Our footsteps stirred the scent of mixed fuels as we wandered, prodding the ground with sticks, seeking anything untouched by fire. I'd see the guys pick up their sticks and smell them once in a while and I called them weirdos. They told me that everything up there smelled different, but apparently my sense of smell wasn't as sensitive as theirs because everything smelled like gas to me.

I heard a clunk against my stick and uncovered a ring. A man's wedding ring? I bent over to pick it up and a bullet whizzed over my head. The sound of the gun and my scream coincided. Joe dove on top of me, driving me into the ground about three inches, face first. I couldn't pull a weapon with his weight on me, let alone breathe. Eagle eye Eddie said he spotted movement just off the road in the woods next to where this property had burned.

Bobby and Alex ran for the truck and sped in the direction Eddie pointed to, taking a sudden left-hand turn into the woods. I heard two shots. Car doors slammed, then the rev of the pickup coming back towards us.

I begged Joe to get off me, but he didn't move until he got an all clear from Eddie. He rolled off me and picked me up in one smooth movement. I had to spit out the debris that was packed into my mouth from his landing. In a single sweep, he cleared my face and ushered me towards Bobby and Alex, who just unloaded the suspected shooter from their truck.

Joe commanded, "Dusty and Rocky, start at the top and walk down to the road below. Find their point of departure. We're going back to the cabins."

Alex asked, "What about this dead guy?"

Joe said, "Get his picture, any ID, prints you can, and leave him up by the road. I'll call the locals on our way."

Eddie drove us and Mickey back to the cabins. Joe talked on the phone during the entire drive back. I realized that my life could have ended a few minutes ago. If they had better aim or I didn't find the ring. Images of the almost hole in my head flashed through my mind, growing increasingly graphic.

Mickey grabbed my hands and asked, "What's happening?"

I wasn't aware that I was rocking and counting as my mind saw my dead body. He shook my hands until I looked at him.

He pulled me over into the middle of the backseat and put his arm around me and said, "You're ok, we got you."

Joe reached back and squeezed my knee while still talking. My head's pressure reached its limit, and the buzzing white noise entranced me. Eddie sped on until we were at the cabins. Mickey multitasked, working on his computer and checking park cameras before our arrival with one arm still hugging me close.

Joe opened my door, took my hand and told the guys to give us 10 before coming back to our cabin. Once inside, he sat on the kitchen chair and pulled me so I straddled him on the chair.

He tried to wipe the caked dirt off my face and started laughing. "I made a pancake out of you, didn't I? I'm not sorry, though."

I stopped him from cleaning me and just held his hands. "I'd be so pissed if I died without more time with you."

He kissed the breath out of me and said, "I agree completely. That's why we stay vigilant every second, especially in New York. I think it's time to head back home. We've had too many close calls. We'll wait for Jeff's team to return to action. The cyber guys have limitations, especially in person."

My emotions skittered the edges of terrified, angry, confused and finally, acceptance. Numerous bad guys were dead within days because of FETCH's presence. My presence escalated the mayhem. I've had so many near-death experiences lately; I don't know how to act.

Joe said, "My dad said he has multiple agencies working on this and gave his blessing to head home. We uncovered the problem, saved the mayor and actually the city of Binghamton. He agrees it's too dangerous for you to be here."

I stood up from Joe's lap and expressed, "I don't want to be a distraction. I just want to help the team."

He stood up and towered over me. "Rachel, are you kidding me? If it wasn't for you, the mayor would be dead. You're an asset, never a hindrance. We'll deal with these crazy assholes, all of them, in time. When it's safe for us and for you. We're not on a timeline. When we get rid of one group, another one will pop up. We've got job security, unfortunately. I just hope that you become less and less known as time goes by."

I hugged him and said, "Me too."

Eddie and Mickey knocked and came in. We hadn't started a fire yet, and it was freezing in here. I warmed my hands in my pocket and discovered the lifesaving ring. I washed it off in the sink and read the engraving on the inside.

"What. Is. This?" I held the ring out to Joe, who read it too.

He asked, "Is that?" Eddie took it from Joe and read the initials. I took the ring back and examined it, hoping for a different message.

"What's the chances someone else could have the exact initials as my parents? So why is my dad's ring in that field? What the hell is happening?"

The room remained quiet for several minutes, except for Mickey tapping on his computer.

Eventually he said, "It's not your parents." He turned the screen so we could all read whose ring it was. "These people match the initials."

I could see the relief on Joe's face, but it was hard for me to accept it so quickly.

"Holy shit, that almost had me bugging out." Eddie laughed and gave me a swipe on the shoulder. "Stop thinking about it. That would be too crazy."

I wasn't convinced despite the oddness of it. I replied, "Yeah, that's too crazy."

Joe's phone rang, and it was the general. He put it on speaker so we could hear the plan. "A few agencies will join you to sort out this mess. You can either stay or go, as I told Joe earlier. I would like you to meet with them before you go, to give them your firsthand account and general feelings about what has happened."

I blurted, "What else do they need to know? Besides a bunch of crazy, misguided assholes who want to kill me but can't shoot for shit and like to blow things up live around here."

JD was quiet for a few seconds, then said, "Rachel, I see your potty returned when you returned to New York."

That remark was ill-timed. "In case you didn't know, someone almost blew my head off. Literally only like an hour ago? I'm sorry if it's caused me to use profanity. Damn it."

Eddie was snickering. Joe stood up, took his father off speaker, and paced around the room to finish the phone call.

Eddie whispered to me, "I hope you're ok with staying because I can't believe Joe would leave in the middle of a mission."

I instantly stood and interrupted Joe. "We can stay as long as needed. I'm ok." I knew if this was a true military mission,

Joe would never leave something halfway taken care of. It would make him crazy.

Joe mouthed, "Are you sure?" I nodded yes, and he walked outside to finish the conversation.

Mickey asked, "You sure about this? It's getting excessive. And I'm not knocking your skills, but you almost got killed a couple times in just a few days. It's ok to want to pack it up, you did your part." Eddie agreed.

"Well, hell yes, I want to leave Binghamton, but I can't hide forever. I'm a target. Everywhere. So, what would you guys do? Can we gain anything by surrendering now? And what about next time?"

Mickey stopped tapping the computer, and Eddie seemed lost in thought, but both remained silent.

"Well?"

Mickey tilted his head and said, "Maybe a wig, some colored contacts, some cheek inserts and some makeup to change the contours of your face would fool facial recognition. And some fake tattoos to cover the ones you have that are visible."

Eddie said, "It's worth a try. Can you get that stuff online?" Mickey scoffed at him and we watched his fingers fly as he procured a new look for me.

Joe returned and mentioned that we'll review the plans once the others return. Peering over Mickey's shoulder, he noticed an array of wigs.

Curious, he asked, "What's happening?"

Mickey replied, "We're devising a plan to outsmart facial and tattoo recognition databases." He turned the computer towards me and requested that I choose a wig.

Before I could, Joe pointed to one and said, "I like that one."

Mickey didn't even wait for me to agree, just clicked on it. And that pissed me off.

"I didn't agree with that. Why do you think you can pick out my wig and I can't? I can't be trusted to make a simple decision about my own damn hair?"

Joe raised his hands and said, "Calm down, tiger." He stood, pointing at the screen. "I picked that one because it's a couple shades from your hair color and this one is too much like how you used to wear your hair in high school and that one matches the style you wore a few years ago. The one I picked is like nothing you've had before."

How could I refute that? I stood with my arms across my chest and glared at him. He smiled at me like it was a gotcha moment, then leaned over and kissed my forehead.

Mickey said, "Decision made, moving on to tattoos."

I said in my most sarcastic tone, "Just order whatever you think is best for me."

The guys brought back subs, and we all gathered in the cabin to eat while Joe briefed us on the plan. "Tomorrow we'll meet with the FBI, Homeland Security and the locals to get everyone up to date, including what happened today. Mickey and Bobby will accompany me to the meeting. We are working under the assumption that we are dealing with two groups that crossed paths. We neutralized the local group. Our focus will be on the group Rachel dealt with in the past."

Eddie asked, "Did we miss something? Did they find the chief's brother-in-law?"

Joe said, "Yes, sorry, my father just told me. Found him dead, looks like a self-inflicted gunshot, but they need an autopsy to confirm, of course, he said it was questionable."

Rocky planned to get some things analyzed at the lab tomorrow, leaving me, Dusty, Eddie and Alex at the cabins.

They didn't ask questions as they finished eating because they trusted Joe as their leader to make the right decisions involving all of us. Or maybe it was a military thing? You were told essential information when you needed to know. I'm not built that way, and I wanted more information.

"What do we do while you're meeting agencies?"

Bobby laughed and said, "I knew you couldn't help yourself."

Dusty said he'd be working on equipment; Alex planned to look at MDS information on chemicals. Eddie said that he and I would work on survival skills.

Bobby said, "It's all covered. Everybody has a job to do."

Joe looked at me and said, "Besides being our local expert and training with Eddie, I'd like you to contact all the people we've trained so far and keep in touch with them on at least a bi-monthly basis."

I felt stupid. "Should I inform them about what's happening? Or just chit-chat?"

Bobby answered, "Let them know we are continuing to deal with a threat and to make sure they have their security teams on alert. Not high alert, but active alert. No short cuts."

Joe nodded and kept eating.

I thought I'd be smart when I asked, "Bobby, do you want to tell Tilly about the threat, or should I?" His cheeks turned pink.

Alex smiled and gave him a thumbs up. "Getting tight with the President's daughter, are you?"

Bobby glared at me. I had to explain. "Look guys, I text with both daughters and his sister Patty frequently. Tilly has mentioned, or actually, she's grilled me on Bobby a few times. I mean, it was obvious when we were there that she wanted to jump your bones."

Bobby pointed to the TV as a diversion. The local news station was talking about the latest developments, showing people walking into the hotel for meetings, when I saw a ghost.

I jumped up and stood closer to the TV and told them, "I know him. He was one of the four guys I killed. How is this possible?"

Joe touched my elbow and asked me to sit down. I shrugged him off and declared it was him. I stared at the TV, waiting in vain for more footage.

"Mickey, find that guy. Find him."

I stood over his shoulder as he found the station and replayed what I saw, stopping it when I pointed to the man I killed two years ago.

He patted my hand that was gripping his shoulder and said, "I'll find out who it is."

Mickey opened a screen with the four monsters and asked which one it was. He compared facial recognition to the man on TV because we've never been able to identify the four men that invaded our lives. No identity meant no searching for relatives or any kind of background information. He found a frontal picture of the current man and compared it to the dead one.

All of us stood as Mickey read aloud his history, including a deceased brother. "Is it his twin? They look so much alike."

Joe stood behind me with his arms around my waist and said, "This is big. If he's like his brother, you may have just found the ringleader."

I leaned back against Joe with an enormous feeling of relief. We sensed it, like this could mark the group's beginning of the end.

Joe told Mickey to send everything he gets to JD. He saluted Joe as he escorted me into the bedroom and ordered me to bed.

DAY FOURTEEN

I woke up alone and reached up to cover my head with the blankets. Why hasn't Joe stoked the fire? I listened for signs of life in the cabin, but the silence scared me into action. I threw off the covers, dressed in yesterday's clothes, and silently approached the door with a gun.

The cabin was empty. On my way to check outside, I threw a few logs in the woodstove. I pulled the curtain aside and noticed two of our vehicles were missing. Alright, what is going on? I called Joe, after two rings it transferred to voice mail. Shit. Why did he leave and why am I so close to having a meltdown? I hurried to other cabins, coat on, extra gun in hand, to check who remained.

The hard frost made the muddy ground crunchy, announcing my footsteps to the next cabin. Locked. Same with the next one. Arriving at Mickey's, smoke billowed from the chimney and his door swung open.

"What the hell is going on? Where is everyone? What happened?"

Mickey put his hands up to stop the verbal assault I hurled his way. "Good morning, Rae. And how are you this chilly morning?"

I briefly wondered if shooting him was an overreaction? He said, "I made coffee, grab a cup and sit down. Eddie is still here, somewhere. The rest are away." His tone signaled for me to grab the coffee and sit beside him.

"At approximately two am, several alarms triggered in the park, all nearing our location. Joe, Rocky, and Bobby left to check it out. They tracked six combatants, who ultimately resisted the call to drop their weapons and identify themselves and succumbed to lethal force." I noticed the six phones sitting on the desk next to his computer.

"Christ, Mickey, you sound like you're giving a report."

He looked up and said, "How did it sound? I'm writing our statement for the Police." Connecting another phone into his computer, he commented, "This civilian stuff can be tricky, especially out here in the woods."

As I got up to see his computer screen, I asked, "Who were they? Was it a legit kill or what?" I surprised myself with that comment and almost felt bad that it didn't even bother me. Like killing people in the woods was as normal as putting your shoes on.

"I'm still getting all their IDs. Three vehicles, six IDs in two trucks, one vehicle with no paperwork in it."

I resumed my seat and inquired about the whereabouts of the guys. "How did I miss all of this?"

Mickey grinned and revealed, "Joe said you were snoring when he mentioned he was leaving. And they went to the addresses on their licenses. They left their IDs in the trucks they came in, parked near the entrance. Eddie was watching your cabin, so you were safe. We've all heard you trying to be quiet in the woods during daylight, so we thought it's best you refrained from assisting."

"Oh, piss off." I knew I couldn't sneak around in the dark, but Joe could've woken me up to stand guard for myself.

Mickey's phone dinged, and he reported the guys were on the way back. "I'm heading back to our cabin to clean up. And then I'll start making breakfast."

Mickey beat me to the door to look outside. Positioned on the stoop, he warned, "Watch out for that icy patch."

I stepped out and said, "Yes, I know what black ice is, Mickey."

My right foot was steady on the ice; however, my left foot went from firmly planted to a high karate kick before I could react. Mickey tried to catch me and ended up under me to break my fall. A bullet hit just above our heads, then another one closer. Mickey put his arms around me and barrel rolled us to the side of the cabin. A third shot came from another direction, then silence.

"That was definitely Eddie," Mickey asserted, then asked, "Are you ok?"

I didn't answer, just stared at him. I almost just died again. How am I ok? Even a cat has to be getting close to catnip heaven. How many is that for me?

I finally said, "How did he get past the sensors?"

Mickey squinted and said, "Good question. Let's go look."

Mickey stood first and peeked around the front of the cabin, then motioned for me to follow him back inside.

Eddie yelled to us before we closed the door. He strolled up with what looked to me like a rocket launcher.

He arrogantly stated, "ID might be tough on him, but here's his phone. I think he was up a tree when we got his friends." He asked Mickey if he had taken a shot, but Mickey shook his head no. Eddie said, "Could have sworn I heard another shot, almost echoed mine."

Mickey grabbed the phone and remarked on the person's height in the tree, missing the sensors. "His ID wasn't in the vehicles. There were only six."

Eddie said, "He was patient, I'll give him that, and that suggests training, like a military sniper."

The guys pulled up and Eddie motioned for them to come to Mickey's cabin. Joe stopped when he saw the bullet holes in the cabin.

Eddie said, "Taken care of. Must have left a combatant in the tree earlier, but he's gone now."

They exchanged incredulous glances, but Mickey assured them that only the sensors near the other guys had activated.

Eddie continued, "This guy had to be ex-military the way he waited it out. And maybe a gun for hire because he didn't risk his mission for his teammates."

He mentioned to Joe that he thought he heard another shot after taking his own. I turned and sat on the couch. This guy watched six people he knew die. He didn't help them, just for the chance of killing me. I was having second thoughts about staying.

Joe ranted, "How the hell are the best of the best getting bested? Despite having all the bells and whistles, they made three attempts on her life." He grasped his head with both hands and stretched his back. "You did better at staying alive when you were on your own. Maybe we're bringing the shit show to you like you say you do to everyone else?"

Bobby interrupted and said, "The situation in Binghamton is clearly more complicated, and as you're aware, desperate and deranged individuals can be more dangerous than a well-executed plan. And let's remember that you can only fight the enemy you can see. Just ask all the wounded warriors."

Mickey acknowledged that although he excels in all things cyber, there are individuals who are more skilled and highly paid to motivate them to engage in black hat hacking. "Most of what they do is unseen. And your dead husband is a perfect example." To clarify, with a grin, he added, "I only use my skills for the good of mankind."

My lack of attention with Michael caused me to feel responsible for all this. He was everything Mickey just described. Sometimes I wished I could just disappear.

Then I thought, "Should we vanish me? Fake my death again?"

It was clear they hadn't considered it, but the wheels turned as soon as I mentioned it.

Joe asked if Mickey got into the shooter's phone yet? "If he is a hired gun, they usually require proof of death to get paid. We can stage that and send it to whichever phone gets the proof."

Mickey said, "I'm working on it as fast as I can. Fuck's sake."

I had to laugh at his frustration.

"I'm cross referencing their call logs and contacts. You were right to assume he wasn't like the others. His phone only has two numbers, with one sitting on this table. So, we have a winner."

Rocky mentioned a dead deer on Rt. 369 that could be used for blood splatter. "Let's go get it."

He and Bobby bolted out the door to retrieve the carcass.

Eddie said, "We'll hold up the deer and shoot it at the level of your head for a realistic splatter pattern against the cabin. Then we stage you."

"Jesus, this is so morbid. But leaving without a real bullet in my head seems like the better plan."

Joe exhaled loudly and said, "I think it's probably the best idea and it'll put them in a different state of mind. Like they've won, so they get cocky. And you know what happens then."

In unison, they said, "You get fucked." I laughed until I cried.

The deer was large and limp, and completely lifeless. Still, I felt guilty when they shot it. They rigged it up so when Eddie shot it with the guy's gun it would be my head level against the cabin, like he made a successful shot with his actual attempt. They squished the deer and let the blood pool where they supposed I would have ended up. It occurred to me I'd have to lie in it. So gross.

Alex was gutting the deer and putting certain parts into a bowl. "This will suffice, even under scrutiny."

"What are you doing with that?" I already knew.

He extended his hand, displaying various tissues and textures, and uttered, "This is your head after a gunshot. So, it's going on your head." I gagged.

No need to inquire about their knowledge of staging the scene. They've all experienced it with teammates and enemies. Too many times, I'm sure. Alex was the medic, so he probably tried to save countless soldiers that had missing body parts, including their heads. I stood watching them work, all from the training they had to protect and serve the USA. They were lucky not to suffer the same level of dysfunction as other veterans.

Alex asked, "You ready for this? It'll be disgusting, not going to lie."

I couldn't protest. It was my idea. "Just tell me what to do."

Joe advised me to change clothes to avoid ruining them. "Change back into your pajamas and throw a FETCH sweatshirt on."

I said, "Good idea. I'll be right back." He followed me to our cabin.

He closed the door and swept me up in his arms. With me being a foot off the ground, I had to wrap my legs around his waist.

He buried his face in my neck and said, "Fucking A, Rae. I want to blow all these fucking psychopaths to fucking Mars." He was shaking and each heavy breath on my neck gave me the shivers.

I couldn't let him fall apart or see that I was about to. "See what New York does to you? It makes you swear."

He lifted his head up to rub his nose on mine. "We won't return after this is over. When we leave, you'll have your closure, even if we destroy the entire city."

He put me down, and I changed back into my pajamas for my photo shoot.

Alex directed me where to lie and how to position my limbs. "Holy Christ, do dead people throw up, because I'm about to."

He fussed at me. "Shut your eyes and focus on something different."

"Right. Well, please suggest what that might be, Alex, when you're smearing guts on my face?"

He said, "Well then, just shut your mouth. Here it comes."

Oh. So gross. They slathered the chosen gut parts and the collected blood to splatter on me. I didn't move one muscle while they were doing this. They took a couple of pictures with the guy's phone and called it a wrap.

Alex told me to tighten up my face so when he wiped it, chunks wouldn't go in any orifice. Joe reached his hand down to help me up. We walked back to the cabin where I stripped outside with Joe holding a towel in front of me. I took the longest, hottest shower I could, which isn't saying much. I washed my hair five times and scrubbed my skin raw. And thought about how much I hated my dead husband for inciting these radical groups by stealing from them. He's responsible for them knowing my name.

Joe sat at our small table with his head in his hands, pen and paper in front of him.

"What are you doing?"

He lifted his head and pulled the chair next to him out. He picked up the pen and tossed it. "Trying to plan the next course of action. You can't stay here. But you have to stay close. I have to act like you died, but still get shit done."

I grabbed his hand and said, "That's a lot to figure out."

He pulled his hand back and rubbed his eyes. "I can't even tell you what seeing you like that did to me. I'm used to close calls, especially in deployment, but in the USA, with you, it sparks different."

Lightheartedly, I bumped his shoulder and quipped, "It's great to see that your wife evokes a distinct response from you."

Joe stood and paced around the room. "Overseas, you know your enemy. You're aware of their intentions and purposes. Not that I agree or understand them, but you can predict the worst. Not one of these anarchists here ever met you. Your involvement in this is unknown to them. You're like a folktale to be destroyed. And then what? I need to communicate that you're innocent and deceased simultaneously."

I stopped him from pacing and suggested, "Why don't you ask the mayor to make a public statement? Then you can tell them you're going to kill them all."

I pulled up to kiss him, but he stopped me short by holding my face in his hands.

"I will kill them all. Without prejudice." He kissed me quick and walked out the door.

My husband changed today. Maybe over the last few days. He knows he can't keep me alive, no matter how skilled he is. He's fighting an entity he doesn't understand, and that frustrates him. Joe's been a dangerous man since I met him, but what he is now is scary. His vibration is ominous. Falling on the ice saved me from a gruesome reality. I returned to the tiny bathroom and cried, and swore at dead people, and at people I've never met, and the ones I knew that I wished were dead.

Twenty minutes later, I heard the familiar heavy footsteps of FETCH coming into the cabin. My puffy eyes and red face told them how I was doing.

Dusty walked over to me and shook my shoulder. "Never give up, never surrender."

"As long as I have a head on my shoulders, I won't. Promise." I put my Boy Scout fingers up and shrugged.

With his hands on his hips, Joe stared at the ceiling, momentarily making me think he would reprimand me for joking. Instead, he started laughing. He walked over and hugged me.

"This, my friends, is what a warrior looks like. She hasn't lost her head or sense of humor."

"Look guys, I'm scared as shit, but I won't give up, and I'll never not fight for my life. You can believe that. Whatever we have to do to get me off their radar and keep shutting them down, I'll do. Whatever. So, what's the plan?"

Mickey put his laptop on the table and showed me my new identity. I was going to hide in plain sight, right here in Chenango Forks. As a woman re-opening a local bar.

"It's logical to assume the place needs work since it's been closed for years. No one should think twice about having contractor vans and delivery trucks stopping by. We can check on you that way."

I was skeptical about the location. "You think that's the best place? A large volume of traffic passes by that location."

Bobby said, "Exactly. Who has the audacity to hide there?"

Mickey continued, "We have to flush up your back story in case anyone gets nosey."

I still wasn't sure. "I'll be living there as well? Is there an apartment inside? Am I supposed to stay there all by myself?"

Joe declared, "That's what we need to discuss. Your companion. My father suggested Jeff come up to stay with you."

I had a hunch he'd say that. "I'd rather have a dog. And Jeff looks too much like you, don't you think?"

Nodding in agreement, Joe proposed, "What if you teamed up with another female agent?"

Flashbacks of my time with Amy Howard spun through my mind. The good, the bad, the questions I still had about her loyalty. She was a badass, though.

"You have someone in mind? What's her background?"

Mickey pulled her statistics up on the screen. "She's a sharpshooter with SWAT in Maryland. We looked at all her physical tests and some videos of her in action. While she is capable, she lacks experience with undercover assignments."

"Why did you pick her if she has no experience in this area?" I would not be happy with the B team.

Alex said, "She was an applicant we considered when we chose our second team and is on the list when we get the third team up. We figured one-on-one training with you would help her when she gets placed and she can definitely handle herself. She's got potential."

Since no one objected, I agreed, "Let's do it."

Mickey offered me a chair and suggested that I take charge of the website work for better understanding. "Any ideas for the bar's name?"

"Can I have a minute to decide? Should it be a theme bar? Sports bar? A bar to attract the crazy zealots around here? No. Wait. I got it. My parents loved Bob Seger. How about Seger Station and we do old rock-n-roll themed stuff?"

As I glanced at Joe, I noticed him deep in thought, contemplating the possibility of someone making a connection.

He surprised me and said, "That sounds like a great name." He picked up his phone and said, "I'm going to call my dad and tell him to get the recruit in motion." He ran his hand over my shoulder as he walked out the door of the cabin.

The guys exchanged a look between themselves and I asked, "What?"

Alex finally answered and said, "Look, we know you've been involved in some gruesome shit, but things have changed. We've always had the scorched earth mentality, but it's escalated to nuclear since this last attempt on your life. Joe and the rest of us fully back any decision you make, even if it involves taking a break. To keep you alive, we are fully into the shoot first and ask questions later mode."

I knew Joe had issued those orders.

Bobby clarified, "We're not going rogue and still have to work within certain rules, but the range is pretty wide. And we're not afraid to exploit the perimeter of said rules."

My lip quivered, and I took a few breaths before I said, "I love you guys. I really do, and I'm sorry if I've made your job harder, which I know I have."

Eddie interrupted me and said, "God, Rachel, don't get all sappy on us."

He punched me in the arm and winked at me. I wiped a couple of stray tears away and turned my attention back to Mickey to plan the bar.

Bobby wrote the statement for the mayor to make. He wrote it by hand and threw it at Mickey before leaving to speak with Joe. I skimmed it before Mickey and admired Bobby's way with words. His points were to make the attempted killers feel stupid, guilty, and outnumbered. I hope it quelled them for a while, anyway.

For the upcoming weeks, Mickey and I arranged for the delivery of various items to the new bar on Route 12 in Chenango Forks. We also decided that the recruit and I needed to look like sisters, which meant me becoming a blonde, and plastering on more tattoos over my current ones to fool any data bases for tattoos.

Mickey sent Bobby's draft to JD and the mayor for approval and legalities.

Joe returned after about an hour with his gear. He said, "We're going to leave all your clothes here, just in case anyone comes looking, it won't look like you moved out. When we leave for the mayor's press conference, you're leaving the same way you left the Whitehouse, in my duffle bag. Then we have to transfer you so you can drive to the bar."

Mickey said, "I've got the paperwork done for cremation, death certificate and also back dated all the applications for liquor license and requests for the bar."

Joe nodded at him, gave me an ear comm, and instructed me, "Ok, Mrs. Cokely, please get in the bag."

I gladly curled up in it so I could hide from everyone. I lost it a few times today and curled up in a dark place by myself was suddenly appealing to me. Everyone grabbed a bag and left the cabin for the press conference. They would

all be present, except me. Joe mentioned that if anyone doubted me getting shot, they would definitely search for evidence at the cabins tonight. "There's plenty of blood splatter staining the door and cabin, as long as they don't DNA test it."

He roughly placed me in the back of a pickup truck. The doors slammed, and the vehicles left the park.

In my ear, Joe told me to unzip the bag, so I'd ready to jump out.

"I hope you're going to slow down."

Eddie replied, "A little. Just roll on your bag when you hit the ground."

I replied, "Jerks."

Joe continued, "The recruit is driving a black transfer van. She'll pull over near the mailbox and pretend to be checking her packages. That's when you jump into her van."

"Well, you make it sound so simple. What could go wrong?" My life has become an action movie.

Shortly after, Joe gave the command, "Go now."

While in motion, I rolled over the box on the pickup, landed on my bag, and rolled to the road's edge. I jumped over a ditch, ran into the woods, and hid behind a tree.

"Check in."

I did, and said, "I'm fine, what's her eta?"

Joe said, "Ten-minute window."

I used the time to confirm the placement of all my weapons after the jump, checked my watch, and waited. Ten minutes. Eleven minutes. Twelve minutes. Well, if this chick can't be punctual, I don't like her already. Fifteen minutes later, I saw headlights.

I told the guys, "Incoming headlights."

Joe said, "Maintain your position. She hasn't contacted us in a few minutes."

Ah, fuck me. "It stopped, going silent."

The van pulled over, but the recruit remained inside. More headlights approached. Since I couldn't get in the van before their arrival, I had to wait. The vehicle stopped next to the van to have a loud chat through open windows, then it pulled away. I waited for a sign that didn't come. The van slowly moved on down the road. I got up and ran further into the woods, up the hill. I reported what happened.

Mickey came on and said, "It's about five miles to the bar. You'll have to hoof it. It's dark enough for cover. The challenge lies in crossing the river unnoticed."

I started moving horizontally on the side of the wooded hill to make my way toward the river. Mickey announced their entrance into the building and informed everyone that they would remain silent for the news conference. I had to sit down. I was alone, in the dark, no comm's, had to remain unseen for five miles, while wondering about the recruit. Today has truly sucked.

On the road below me, headlights of three vehicles sped toward the park. Only two routes led to the park, this being one of them. It could be anyone, but I had the notion they were looking for me, or evidence of my dead body. What could I hope this press conference accomplishes?

And how the hell am I getting across the river without using the bridge? I wonder if I can use the bottom of the bridge? I sat back down and opened my bag. I thought it was Joe's stuff, but he packed it for me. No spiderman's hands in there, but some rope, duct tape, more weapons, a wig, a radio, bottle of water and some protein bars. I've had it with these damn wigs. I mean they haven't saved me yet. Unless they have, who knows? I pulled the wig on and kept going. After a brief pause under cover, I sprinted across the road and tumbled down the nearby hill next to the bridge. There

was a rocky ledge under the bridge, and thankfully, the water was low. Rocks jutted out of the water at various points, extending to the opposite side. I could probably wade across instead of trying to attach myself to the bottom of the bridge and still stay hidden under the bridge. I dipped my hand in the freezing water and worried about getting hypothermia from going in waist-deep. Looks like I'll find out.

I scanned across the river and noticed that I could remain partially concealed by walking along the river for at least a mile before I would need to cross and approach the road, Route 12. I debated, but left my boots on and waded across. I slung my duffle bag up on my shoulders like a backpack. I preferred not to discover my weapons' functionality issues after being submerged. The water reached just above my knees for most of the way. Instead of stopping, I turned right and continued walking along the river bed. When I could, I ran. The small, abandoned campground I forgot about gave me plenty of privacy to run, getting me closer to my target while still hidden.

Mickey was back in my ear telling me, "Doing great. You've got about."

I stopped him. "Don't bother telling me how far I have in distance. What's the walking time until I cross the road?"

"Stay on your side until I tell you to cross. Does that work?"

I had to smile. "Yes, that works." Route 12 is really busy. I was in the ditch, hiding more than I was walking. I finally reached the bar that would serve as my residence for a while and hoped the heat was working.

"You're a go to cross whenever you can. Back door entrance, key is in your bag."

I waited for countless cars to pass, then quickly crossed the road and entered from the back.

I locked the door behind me and leaned against it to catch my breath for a minute. I led with my gun, turning on the lights as I checked the entire bar. I placed stools in front of the three doors and finally removed my duffle bag from my back. My legs were numb from the river and running, so I took my boots off and shimmied out of my jeans that were wet up to my crotch, and laid them over a bar stool. I emptied the contents of my bag on the bar and changed into dry clothes.

Mickey was in my ear telling me that there were cameras everywhere except in the bathroom.

"You couldn't tell me that before I changed?"

Laughing, he mentioned the two bags sitting on the bar. "Best we could do short notice. Knives and some weapons are in the kitchen area. Get familiar with them. The fridge in there is half full. Try not to eat it all tonight." Even though he joked, I can sense that they're all equally nervous as me. "Joe will call you later. Rest up."

And with that, I was alone, tired and hungry.

Two bags sat at the end of the bar. One contained hair color, makeup, fake tattoos, wigs and glasses. The other had some concert t-shirts, jeans and jewelry. I had to leave behind my wedding rings with Joe. It's remarkable how something like that can elicit such deep feelings. Shit like this makes me hate these nuts and my dead husband even more. I'm glad he's dead and I'm glad I killed him before he killed me. I wish the aftermath wasn't so challenging, but that's my reality. Recent weeks have taken a toll on my spirit and I know I need to get my head on straight for whatever happens next.

I headed to the kitchen and got the knives and walked around the bar and stashed them in strategic places. I strategically positioned guns by each door and behind the bar in two places. It'll be my fault if someone gets me before I get them.

I wonder where the recruit is? I keyed my comms and asked Mickey about her. He didn't answer, and I didn't keep trying him. They're in public, so he can't appear like he's talking to someone in his ear. I went to the kitchen, made a sandwich for myself, and opened a beer. I checked the office area after I ate and found a sleeping bag. The idea of using that as a bed indefinitely was unappealing. Then I considered the awful places the team has had to sleep and cooled my jets. But still. It sucked.

The pool table seemed like a suitable sleeping spot. At least it was better than the dirty floor. I moved some weapons to the pockets of the pool table and laid out the sleeping bag for later. The place had about ten TVs, so I manually turned one on. No cable service, of course, but it picked up local channels. I tuned in to catch the breaking news banner across the bottom and the mayor interrupting the show. Next to her stood various officials and Joe. My Joe. He's the one who inspires me to live.

Michelle Devine informed the public about recent events and described the perpetrators. The screen showed pictures of deceased criminals, cautioning against repeating their actions. She introduced the people beside her and mentioned that every agency mentioned had resources to apprehend the criminals. Also standing near her was the monster's brother, looking as offended and determined as everyone else who stood with her.

Next, she introduced Joe. He announced my senseless death and detailed what happened two plus years ago to me because of Michael. Joe repeated several times that I was innocent and not involved in any theft that my husband may have perpetrated. He stated he wouldn't rest until they brought those involved to justice. With a menacing look, he walked off the stage.

Officials on stage explained their roles and displayed additional pictures of individuals they are searching for. A bunch of them. I took a picture of each one with my phone, then I grabbed another beer and the hair color. Shall we determine if blondes experience greater enjoyment?

A half hour later, my hair and eyebrows were almost platinum. That alone should throw anyone off, but I added some temporary tattoos around my neck and hands in case I had any unexpected guests in the morning. I needed another beer, as the first two failed to relieve tonight's tension.

I turned on neon beer signs for night lights, checked doors, and looked out windows before getting on the pool table with the sleeping bag. I didn't feel quite safe enough to get inside of it yet. With a gun and knife in my hands, I stared at the ceiling, waiting for Joe's call.

I wondered if the original group would even care that I wasn't involved in Michael's scheme, but I'm glad Joe told them. They didn't try to uncover the truth. They just wanted revenge and me dead. Much like the situation with my uncle. It was too much to hope he was dead. And now that Joe announced my death, I wonder if he'll come around to see for himself. I hope he does so I can kill him.

DAY FIFTEEN

I slept on and off throughout the night and finally woke up at 5:30 to Joe's phone call.

"Good morning, my love. I'm sorry I couldn't call earlier. Mickey double-checked the line for security. Did you sleep?"

Hearing his voice was wonderful. "Hi. I slept on and off. I'm ok."

He sighed and said, "The recruit said someone followed her after she slowed down to pick you up, so she drove back to a pizza place on Front Street and picked up more pizzas to supposedly deliver. They followed her again, so she's out of the running on this assignment. We're working on someone else. But for now, you're solo." What could I say?

"Ok, I get it. Please keep me updated so I don't shoot whoever knocks on the door."

He laughed and said, "Mickey will send you a list of the deliveries he scheduled. They start tomorrow and remember that there are cameras everywhere, so we can see if something goes sideways. Just hang tight for a couple of days until we have another plan."

"Don't worry about me. You guys keep looking for the bad guys. I'll be busy cleaning and organizing the bar."

"Ok, babe, I'll talk to you soon. I love you, Rae."

I smiled when I said, "And I love you."

When I first caught sight of myself in the bathroom, I almost pulled my gun. I washed my face and was careful not to let water drip on my new tattoos. I'd like them to stay crisp for as long as they could.

After freshening up, I double-checked the doors and cracked open the blinds on the windows. As per a usual bar, there weren't too many windows, anyway. A commercial size window that didn't open was by the front door. The others were in back - one in each restroom, kitchen, and office. Barred windows adorned the back and side doors. In the dim light, I ventured outside through the back door onto a gravel area permeated with the stench of discarded cigarette butts. Tall weeds grew up through the gravel and beyond that were bushes that grew into trees and tall trees covered in vines. Past that, about a football field away, were houses. I walked to the building's side where a privacy fence connected to the bar, hiding the garbage dumpster. To access it, they need to drive around.

I sure would like some coffee. I keyed Mickey up on my comms and asked him about that. "You'll be getting a grocery delivery today. I'll add that to the list."

"Thanks." I had another thought after he confirmed it was from Walmart. I gave him a list of items to send, including quality toilet paper.

I wore the clothes and wig that were left for me. It still seemed strange to have hair brushing against my shoulders after several years of me shaving half my head. At least if someone tried to pull my hair now, they'd end up with a wig and not me.

I turned on the TV for company and searched for cleaning supplies. It was cleaner than expected, given the place was for sale. It had more of a layer of dust over everything rather than grime. Lucky me. Hours flew by and by noon I'd cleaned every surface. While I was behind the bar, an explosion on TV caught my attention. Before turning around, I took a deep breath in anticipation of what had exploded, hoping I recognized nothing belonging to FETCH. The reporter was saying the explosion happened about fifteen minutes ago. The noise was caught on a nearby resident's security camera and they called it in. Their investigation was just beginning. I couldn't discern its location, nor did they give an address to the burning house.

I called Joe and keyed Mickey on comms. Neither answered. The reporter stated their return would occur once a crew arrived for a live broadcast. The soap opera watchers wouldn't be happy about the interruption. I came from behind the bar, sat on a barstool, and waited. Instead of just sitting there, I perfectly lined up all the barstools. How far was the house that exploded? Why was someone filming it? Where were the guys? They heard me yelling at the TV, so they returned to report the house that exploded was at the end of a dead-end road in Port Crane. Fire trucks, pickups and SUVs sped past the reporter to the scene. I think one of the SUVs was FETCH. I sent another message to Mickey, asking if everyone was okay, and received a click in return. Thank God.

If they're only going there now, maybe they didn't blow it up. So, who did? The reporter wasted time talking until they gave him a paper. He read it and as soon as he started speaking; the sirens grew louder, drowning him out and police vehicles used their bull horns to tell all the news stations to evacuate the road immediately. The camera man kept filming the emergency vehicles coming down the road, away from the fire. What in the world? The reporter jumped in the van, leaving the door open so they could keep reporting and filming. I keyed Mickey again and said he better answer me. I got another click in response to my request. Dammit. I could hear another explosion in the background through the TV. Was it a trap? The hurried departure suggests that someone had already figured it out before they faced another explosion.

A few minutes later, they were all gathered in a parking lot for the highway department, still filming and talking, speculating mostly. Who, what, and why?

Three loud knocks on the front door drew me away from the circus. I lowered the volume and headed towards the door. I peeked out the window and saw a UPS truck, then opened the door. The driver had a large box on his dolly and stated he had three additional boxes. One by one, he rolled them inside, left them at the bar's center, and wished me a good day before departing. It was like Christmas opening the boxes. They held bar and kitchen supplies, toiletries, dry goods, small snack bags, more clothes, an inflatable bed, pillows and window film. My delivery would keep me busy for hours and keep me from sitting in front of the tv watching people guess what was going on. I'd just wait to hear it from reliable sources.

I spent an hour organizing supplies. I checked my watch every five minutes after that, and finally, after another 30 minutes, I had to call Joe.

He answered, "Yes, sir, I can give you a briefing now." He sounded stressed.

"I'm sorry, I couldn't take it anymore, Joe. What's happened?"

He told me, "The house and grounds stored a large quantity of munitions. Military grade, all of which was destroyed. Once the area is clear for more explosions, we'll attempt to identify the weapons for serial numbers and origin of the weapons supply. Still attempting to locate the owner.

Despite the lack of information, there have been no reports of casualties. I'll call to report more, when I know more."

He hung up before I could say anything else. It's no fun being dead. People aren't supposed to talk to you.

I suddenly got a new appreciation for military spouses. They live for years on little to no information from their hero loved ones. I'm going bonkers being sidelined for one day.

Two knocks on the door. I peeked out and saw a woman unloading her minivan with bags. Must be my Walmart delivery. I grabbed some cash to give her a tip before she hurriedly got back in her van and left. Was she scared of my looks and the bar? I got all the bags in one haul and was delighted to see my favorite ice cream, moose tracks included. With groceries stored, most of the day lay ahead. Acquiring the skills to tend bar would be advantageous as a bar owner. I stumbled upon a bartender's guide behind the bar and studied it while enjoying a beer.

Around six, I had to get outside. The back was private, given the neglected state it was in. The front, however, was an open book to Route 12. Hiding in plain sight has given me a dose of anxiety, but I have to act like I belong here, so I didn't bolt behind the bar when cars drove by. I cleared a spot by the back door to remove the smell of damp, decayed cigarette butts. I took a stool out and sat there until it got completely dark. The temperature seemed to drop twenty degrees once the sun was gone.

I grabbed another beer and cooked a burger on the flat top grill. I made a side salad and put half of it on my burger. I sat at the bar to eat and watched the local news. The banner across the bottom of the TV reported an ongoing investigation of an explosion, no details available. I wondered if they were keeping it hushed up. Nothing else exciting happened today in Binghamton.

After I washed my dishes, I blew up my new bed with the foot pump that came with it. I rearranged the office to hide my sleeping spot. Then I wondered what shape the attic was in. That might make a better bedroom. I stopped inflating the mattress and used a bar stool to reach the pull-down door. The string only hung about six inches from the top. I stood on my tippy toes to grab it and pulled the stairs down. I used my phone as a flashlight and climbed the stairs to look around. Surprisingly, a light switch inside the attic lit up the space. I stood upright amidst the roof supports, walked to the attic's end, and found a tacked-up cardboard. I pulled it away from the hidden window. It was big enough for me. An emergency exit if I needed one. I think this will be my bedroom.

I deflated the mattress so it would fit up the stairs, then blew it back up and threw my sleeping bag on it. The light switch had an outlet, so I added a small office light to it. I needed a long string to pull down the stairs, not the barstool beneath.

Good Lord, it was only 8:30pm. I wanted to talk to Joe, or my mother-in-law, or any of the team, hell I'd talk to my least favorite brother-in-law, Jeff, if I could. But here I sit, supposedly dead, again. I wonder where my Uncle Roger is and if he heard the news. I bet he'll come looking for the truth now that he knows where my last location was. I hope I see him first this time. Something to look forward to. Then I'll kill him.

I played pool and drank beer until around midnight. Afterward, I checked all doors for the tenth time, grabbed water, and went up to my new bedroom, convincing myself it wasn't such a terrible arrangement. I wrongly thought that sleeping in a bar attic was better than being with my warm, handsome husband. And that my life, after my parents died, was boring, and now I'm not bored. It was flattering to receive so much attention. Ha. I cried myself to sleep.

DAY SIXTEEN

The sound of the bar phone reached me through the floor. I scrambled out of my sleeping bag and practically slid down the attic stairs to just miss the call. I grabbed the phone and went to the bathroom, knowing it would ring again if I didn't bring it with me.

"Seger Station." I answered as I was pulling up my pants.

"Jess, I'll be there to pick you up in ten minutes to go file the papers for the bar. Make sure you bring the important documents with you, OK?" Her voice had a familiar tone to it.

"Oh, ok, great. Give a knock on the door when you arrive." She hung up, and I called Joe, then everyone. No answers. In front of the camera, I raised my hands in a questioning gesture.

Leaving without explanation was not an option for me. I collected my belongings and stashed them in my on-the-go bag, then promptly surveyed the bar to locate the places where I had concealed my weapons and loaded up with as many weapons and bullets as possible.

It was less than ten minutes later when an old pickup with dark tinted windows pulled up and beeped the horn. I specifically said knock on the door. This is fishy. They beeped again while slowly driving past the bar where the dumpster was. Why bother tinting the windows of an old truck? If I walked over to the side door, they'd notice me looking out. I hurried back to the attic for a better view from my little window.

Holy Christ, it was Amy Howard who got out the driver's side door. She walked behind the truck and gestured with a horizontal cut, then a fist. Like, stop and don't move. From my angle, I could see there was a passenger, but that's it. Amy banged on the side door, shouting Jess's name. I wasn't even breathing at this point. She glanced back at the pickup for guidance. The window rolled down, and a jowly faced man sneered at Amy. They talked for a second, then she rounded the truck. She briefly stood behind the truck, mimicking a gun with her hand and firing at the passenger. Jesus, do I just shoot someone at her command? Do I trust her?

The man inside the truck flung his door open, holding a gun, and yelled at her. I couldn't make it out, only caught his voice and could sense they weren't friends. She gestured at the bar and he emphatically pointed for her to return to the truck. I'd have to break out the window to shoot him. Moving towards him from behind the truck, she kept herself involved in conversation. He raised his voice again and pointed his gun. I tapped the window, making him look up, giving her time to grab his gun and shoot him. She pushed him backwards into the truck and shot him again before fully loading him into the cab. She turned and waved before she nonchalantly got back in the pickup and slowly drove back toward Greene. What the hell just happened?

I stood in the attic for a minute, trying to plan my next move. Someone knew I was here. But which group were they associated with? How did Amy get involved? More importantly, how much time did she buy me? Guess the jig is up and I've got to move. I hurried through the bar, grabbing guns, knives, and tools to fill my bag. I put my

Kevlar vest on under my coat and stepped out the front door. Pretty sure I looked like a short, bulky hiker headed toward Chenango Forks.

I waited forever for a break in the heavy morning work traffic to cross the road. I retraced my previous route through the field to the river. At 8:00 am, I reached the old campground and broke into the middle cabin. What a start to a day. And where was my team? I sat on the floor and tried to plan it, work and time it, until it occurred to me that my team didn't answer because they couldn't. Because something bad happened. Because of me.

I rocked myself to calm down. I had to stop this negative spiral I was in and think positive. The team was ok. They were elite soldiers. I was the odd one, if you will. I knew options were pretty limited to ask for help from others. After all, I was dead. I had only myself to rely on.

I peeked out the windows periodically and didn't spot a single person all day. I left the cabin only once during the day, as I needed to pee. I waited until it was dark to follow the river bank all the way to Kenyon school. During the journey, I contemplated the hazards of asbestos and the duration of exposure required for adverse effects. I'm sure I could find some places that looked intact. Maybe the garages? It took under 30 minutes to arrive and access the garage.

My pants were heavy with river water, my boots were squishy, and I was freezing. When will it get warm up here? In just a few years, my blood became southern. I used my phone's light to inspect debris in the garage and found a tarp and shelving for a makeshift tent. I took my boots and pants off and hooked them on a nail on the wall to dry. At least my hot breath might warm me up under the tarp.

I curled up in the fetal position and hoped that the tracking devices would lead the team to me. But what if it didn't? What if they were dead? What if Uncle Roger, that son of a bitch, killed them all? My Joe. What if I never saw him again? How could I just wait? Tucked up in a ball?

After an hour, I put my semi dry pants and shoes back on and headed outside. I needed to move. I jogged along a tree line back down the river and stood there. Thinking. How was this going to end? What was FETCH's plan?

I heard it before I saw it. A helicopter. I ducked into the bushes and watched as it landed in the field behind the school. I never flinched while looking at it, so I can't explain how the masked soldier surprised me.

He grumbled, "Time to go, Rachel."

The tall man grabbed my bag, then me around the waist and hoisted me to him at his hip as he ran to the helicopter. My instincts finally kicked in and I elbowed him in the chest.

He dropped me, grabbed my arm and grumbled, "The General ordered your extraction. Now keep moving."

Doing as he instructed, I took double the number of steps he did. Thank God the door was open because he hurled me through it so hard, I nearly flew out the other side. I got up and sat in the seat and he strapped me in. The instrument lights provided the only illumination in the helicopter. As soon as I got my bearings, I pointed my pistol at him and asked who he was.

He sneered, "A friend." I wasn't sure.

"Take off your mask and hood."

My gun didn't faze him. He closed his door and signaled for me to do the same. I finally noticed another figure in the helicopter, besides the pilot. An elderly man, in an equally aged helicopter. Damn, I hate these things.

The pilot zig zagged down the river, a little too low for my comfort, and definitely too fast. The man sat on the end seat of his side, his gun on his lap, finger still at the trigger. I waited for a minute before asking again. "Well?"

He didn't look at me when he answered in a gravelly voice. "Jonathan ordered you home."

My stomach flipped, my mind raced, and my heart sunk. How could I possibly think this was my dad just because he called him Jonathan? He has passed away, and JD surely has acquaintances who refer to him using his first name. Betty occasionally refers to him that way.

"You still didn't answer my question." He leaned forward and grabbed a parachute bag and handed it to me.

"Put this on. You'll be leaving with it. Someone else will pick you up."

I knew I wouldn't get answers from him, or even JD. But I'll definitely ask JD.

The man across from me yelled, "I'm Alfred. I worked on this bird, so it's safe." He paused and added, "Enough." I considered jumping now. He handed me a headset and nodded his head at me. I wore them and he assured, "No need to worry about crashing. Once repaired, I must ride in them, a practice I've upheld for quite some time."

I asked, "How long?"

He said he was part of the first UTT helicopter in Nam. I tried to do the math for his age and wondered what UTT was.

He read my mind and said, "That stands for Utility Transport Helicopter. The Army's first armed helicopter."

I'm thinking he must have been a badass.

After another few minutes, he said, "I understand you're quite ingenious with survival skills. We'll have to have a talk sometime. We had to manufacture a wide range of devices back then on that bird. Trial and error with lives at stake. We perfected our guns as best we could, improvised where we had to, just to stay alive. You might appreciate some stories like that."

I liked this guy. "I look forward to hearing about what you did. Thanks."

The grumpy man said, "You're awfully talkative, Alfred."

He answered without hesitation, "Anything for Roly's daughter."

Before I could respond, the man snatched my headphones off my head and pushed at the parachute I had on my lap. "Put it on."

I put the parachute on my back and tightened it so much it hindered my breathing. I didn't want it to slip off. He gave me a quick reminder of what to do after I jumped. He may need to push me. I think I'd prefer to listen to Alfred's story than jump by myself in the dark. He glanced at his watch and informed me I had an hour for rest. Take a nap. That's the dumbest thing I've ever heard. I hate helicopters. I don't know who I'm with, but they're telling me I have to jump out of the helicopter that I hate. Rest would not happen. I'll just sit here and let my imagination run wild. This wasn't in my plan.

"Where's my husband?"

He replied instantly. "Working." I believed him.

I fixated on my father's words about Jonathan coming for me. Trust him. No questions. The stranger referred to the General as Jonathan, reminding me of how my dad addressed him. What if they faked their deaths, like I've done? Except they were way better at it. Would they really leave me? Before, I couldn't comprehend their motives. Now, I might.

There was only darkness out every window. I pressed my face to the window, looking below the bird, still black.

"Where are the lights?" I wrangled the headset back and said, "Don't think I'm jumping into the water."

He said nothing, and I started undoing my parachute. He grabbed my hand and said we were over the mountains in Virginia. I would be jumping into a field soon.

"Why do I have to jump? Why can't you land? This seems stupid. Just land in the damn field. I can't jump by myself."

And off I started into a panic attack. I tore off the parachute and struggled to open the door for fresh air. He grabbed my pants and pulled me back into the seat. He chopped his hand in front of me, as if that would calm me. Ha. He asked the pilot to seek clearance for landing. The pilot did as he asked and announced we'd be landing, per my request.

"Was that so damn hard? No! Just land this bird in a deserted field and let me out in the middle of nowhere, jack wagon, Virginia. Sounds like a brilliant plan."

The man looked straight ahead. I stared at him, searching for any part of him that wasn't covered in material or the hard, fitted mask he wore. I wondered if he had known my dad also, if this was something like he used to do. I wanted to ask. Instead, I turned my head as the heaviness of missing my parents settled in my chest.

Alfred yelled, "You'll be fine, kid. Go with your instincts." He might give too much credit for what I inherited from my father.

The pilot gave notice of landing, in a measurement I didn't know. Why can't they just say minutes or miles? We landed smoothly, but I stayed put until he directed me to leave.

"Get out."

Alfred gave me a thumbs up as I exited into the night. The grumpy masked man pointed into the dark. He said a male and female driving an Explorer would meet me and take me to base. I needed to walk to the road, which if I ran, I could make it in twenty minutes. So, he said. He handed me a large flashlight and nudged me away from the helicopter.

I grabbed his coat sleeve and asked, "Why?"

He shook me off and slid the door shut in my face without answering, and they took off, sending debris everywhere. I crouched down and waited for the wind to fade away. For someone who came to my rescue, he was a jerk.

I repositioned my backpack and starting running in the direction he told me. I made it to the road in fifteen minutes and sat hidden from view. It was a dirt road without traffic in either direction. Am I in the right spot? I got up after a few minutes and walked south, according to my compass. After another ten minutes of walking, I got pissed. What happens when I run out of dirt road? Or some local cops want to search me and my huge stash of weapons on my back? Dammit, I fucking hate all these crazy ass people that think killing me, one person will change anything in their stupid, misguided lives. I sound as crazy as they are, except I'm on the right side of it.

Approaching lights. Finally. They flashed the lights on and off as they slowly neared. I stood off to the side, gun in hand, flashlight aimed at the ground. The couple got out of the explorer, identified themselves, their ranks and stated General Cokely requested my presence in South Carolina. I used my flashlight to search the SUV before I got into the backseat. Beside me was a bag with two burgers, fries, and a bottle of water.

The woman driving said, "We should have you home in about six hours."

I ate my food and nodded off thinking about my parents, and my old life. Wondering if I'll always be running for my life. Would it change if I left FETCH?

DAY SEVENTEEN

My head bounced off the side window and woke me up. It was still dark out. I looked out the window, hoping to glimpse something familiar. Thankfully, I did and estimated I'd be on base in ten minutes or less. The closer we got, the more nervous I got. I leaped into the SUV's cargo area and peeked out. The woman glanced in the rear-view mirror and inquired about my well-being. Mentally; I snapped and told her I wasn't okay; how could I be? Out loud, I told her not to stop for anything or anyone.

Two vehicles were waiting at the gate when we arrived. My husband's brother Jeff stood outside the one that held JD. I don't know if I'll ever claim him as my brother-in-law, but he is dependable. Uniformed men were in the other vehicle. They appeared to be MPs. Jeff approached and opened the door for me. I switched to the back seat and pushed him aside to leave.

I ducked my head back in and said, "Thanks for the ride."

Jeff grabbed my bag off my shoulder and told me to get in.

I snarled back, "No shit. Should I get in?"

He gently shoved me toward the SUV and said, "You're a real pain in the ass, ya know?"

As I got in, I said, "Yeah, thanks anyway, though."

JD grabbed my hand for a quick tug and said, "Nice to see you in one piece. I believe you'll be better off here, out of harm's way. The situation in Binghamton is far too complicated to ensure your safety." His unspoken words implied I am a liability.

Jeff weighed in from the front seat. "Don't get all huffy. What he means is that Mom said she wanted her shopping buddy home."

JD covered my hand and said, "Something along those lines. There was no way to keep you safe, and to keep FETCH working. The backup plans fell through and we didn't anticipate the level of corruption in the leaders there. You can help from here." He put his hand up to stop me and said, "Later. We'll discuss this later."

JD told me training events had increased at base and that if I encountered anyone, especially someone who's never talked to me before, I was to ask if they had a pet. A black swan is the answer. They left me at the cabin, telling me to rest, promising to return. JD added, "Jeff will stay at base with you, and you two will play nice." I held my tongue.

I inspected the house thoroughly and strategically positioned weapons, just like before. It made me feel better when I was alone, so I did it. I've been alone here many times, but I never felt this spooked. Then, I bumped up the thermostat, showered, and went to bed at 8:00am.

I glanced at the clock and saw it was 4:20 pm. Just as I was about to rise, I heard heavy footsteps on the stairs. Banging on my door seconds later was Jeff. Not knocking, banging. I knew it was him, but he announced himself anyway. "I'll be there in a moment". He made as much noise retreating down the stairs.

I put on a sweatshirt, leggings and thick socks on to join him. He was in the kitchen, already eating the pizza that he brought. He grabbed a beer and plate and slid them towards me at the bar. I indulged in both without talking. Three slices and two beers later, we moved to the living room.

"So, it was a real shit show up there. Is it worth it?"

I was confused. "Is what worth it? Standing up against a group of assholes? Living my life? Breathing? What specially do you mean?"

He makes me mad just looking at him. Even though he looks so much like Joe, he's much harder.

He took a long sip of beer before answering. "I guess all of it. You could disappear into witness protection. Leave the country, go to some tropical island. Never look back."

I threw a pillow at him. "You want me to leave Joe like that? You don't like me, I get it, I bring the shit show with me, but your brother loves me and I him." Then it hit me. "Wait, vanish, like my parents? What do you know about them? Is that who picked me up?"

Jeff rose from his seat and retrieved two more beers. As he handed me one, he asked, "Did you hit your damn head lately? Memory loss? Your parents are dead. As in never coming back. Why would you think otherwise?"

"Because the man who picked me up called your father Jonathan, like my dad did."

He looked at me like I was stupid. "That is his name. And his lateral, long-time colleagues call him that, just like your father did." He tossed the pillow and questioned, "Are you truly prepared for the ongoing battle with these groups?"

I hugged the pillow and asked, "How many times have you deployed? Fighting the same opponents, because the battle persists, and is still worth fighting? That's my intention. To keep fighting. Because they keep bringing the fight to me, and mine," I waited a beat and said, "What would you do if you were me?"

He gasped and said, "That's a fate worse than death." I stared him down until he added, "I'd fight for my life."

I held my beer up to clank against his, and we nodded together. Jeff turned on the TV and found an old John Wick movie to watch. He smiled into his beer and said, "See if you can pick up any tips."

Jeff's phone vibrated with a text. He shook his head and handed it to me. "Thanks for looking after my dog while I'm away. She's the best, just needs a lot of food and exercise, or she gets wound up." I typed back, "She misses her master." Overwhelmed by emotions, I went to bed before Jeff could pick on me about it.

DAY EIGHTEEN

Before Jeff woke up, I was already up, brewing coffee and making a grocery list. JD arrived at the door before the coffee was half finished. Jeff rushed into the room upon hearing his voice, like he was running late for a test.

JD sat at the table and motioned for me to join him. I didn't even sit before I asked, "Was that my dad who picked me up?"

He looked sad when he asked, "Are you ok? Were you injured?" Jeff snickered behind me. I flipped him off while I kept my eyes on JD.

"Well?"

"No, Rachel," JD replied. "That wasn't your father, but I'm not at liberty to disclose his identity. Just know it was a trusted friend."

JD likely categorized my additional questions as confidential. He guards that vault tightly. I asked a question he could answer.

"Ok, now tell me about the team. Is everything ok?"

JD answered, "Everyone is fine, very busy. They're still working under the assumption you're dead, at least up there."

The coffee signaled it was done, and I poured three cups. I sat with JD at the table and told him everything that had happened since we arrived in Binghamton. When I mentioned Agent Amy Howard's sudden appearance and her subsequent shooting of her companion, his expression became blank. For several seconds he stared into his coffee mug before asking me a million questions about how she contacted me, how long it took to arrive, the details of the pickup and the man.

"Wait, JD. Did you not know she was there? How is that possible?"

He shook his head, glanced at Jeff and told him to get Mickey on the details and tracing her call.

A stickler for details, he requested me to repeat the event, ensuring nothing escaped my memory. I trained with him for weeks before starting with FETCH and he was calling on all that to jog my memory for any puzzle piece that's important. He wrote notes, drew diagrams and grilled me like an expensive attorney.

Jeff listened to all of it without interrupting and made breakfast without a peep. Around ten, I needed a pee break. Upon my return, Jeff sat at the table with his notebook before him. He was scribbling his own recollection of what I said in the correct order timeline. It was somewhat impressive. Sometimes I think I should give him some slack, since Uncle Roger almost killed him, and that's all on me.

JD said goodbye to whoever he was talking to on the phone. His ears were red.

I asked him again, "JD, are my parents really dead? Like, forever, not like what I've done?"

He leaned forward and rubbed his middle finger up the bridge of his nose. "If they aren't, they have truly become ghosts. I've not had one inclination in all these years that they're alive. I wish I could say different. I think if they were, your situation would have resurrected them."

Jeff added his two cents. "And the death toll around you would be higher than it is."

I flopped down in the chair. Jeff said, "As long as his brother is unaccounted for, he'll stay dead. I mean, if he isn't." JD's look was as powerful as a slap to Jeff's face.

With nostrils flared, JD grumbled, "The Sampson's are dead. Period." He gathered his papers to leave and then said, "By the way, Mr. Alfred requested a visit with you. He's resting up today, so we'll coordinate another time."

Jeff looked put off. "Why would a war hero choose to spend time with you?"

I flicked him off and said, "Because I'm that special."

He scoffed, remarking, "Yeah, special, but not in a good way."

It was hard to tell if JD was mad or amused at our banter. Prior to leaving, he instructed, "Go to the box and exert some energy, both of you."

Alone, Jeff and I sat at the table. He suggested that if they faked their deaths, there were no other possibilities.

"Our parents were best friends, and he was my godfather. Did you know that?" He didn't wait for me to answer. "Your father helped me early in my training. He was the most capable man I ever met. He trained you, though you were unaware of it then. I believe it's what has kept you alive."

He pounded his fist on the table and said, "Go get changed. Let's go work out." He paused and added, "The obstacle course is calling your name."

As I ran up the stairs, I chided, "Ha, you aren't ever getting your name back on that board. My time will eternally outshine yours. Every birthday and pound make you slower."

We walked to the box together with him trash talking the entire way. He had a much harder look than Joe, and gray streaked his temples. He was an inch taller at 6'6" and twenty pounds heavier than Joe, and I have no idea how I beat this time, other than my scrawny weight of 120 was easier to move around than his 260. JD and Betty raised five of South Carolina's most handsome and capable men. Joe trusts his brother implicitly. I have the same sentiment, but he irritates me more than anyone else.

Upon entering the box, I drew a few stray eyeballs until Jeff ominously appeared behind me. Then they all minded their business.

He grumbled, "Make sure I can see you at all times."

I elbowed him in the gut and said, "Don't you mean make sure you can see me? You're the bodyguard."

I walked off to practice the individual events of the obstacle course, just in case we raced each other.

I grabbed my boxing gloves off the wall after wrapping my hands. Jeff strolled over to tie them on me. I let him.

He told me, "Be sure to practice your kicks too, just in case your pitiful punches don't take them down." I punched him in the stomach when he wasn't ready for it.

His response was, "Like I said, practice your kicks."

I muttered he was an asshole to his back. He had a point. Guys his size would laugh at me. But I wouldn't fight fair with guys his size either. Punches and kicks to their joints and balls would save me, not hitting their faces or trunks.

After an hour, Jeff asked if I wanted to attempt the situation house. We left the box and walked toward the house and our cabin. I didn't want to, but I also didn't want to appear weak to him.

"If you want to, otherwise I'm ready for dinner."

He mulled it over before he said, "We never went to the store. Guess I'll take a shower before I head out. I can pick something up for dinner." He took another step and added, "And no, you can't come with me. I don't need your trouble." Damn, that actually hurt my feelings.

After we got back, I completed the grocery list and left it on the counter for him while I showered. He was gone when I returned downstairs. I did a quick run through of the house, checking and rechecking where I put weapons. As safe as I felt here, history shows me to never be too careful.

I didn't ask JD if I should stay on base and pretend to be dead here. Can I go out with my wigs and glasses? A polite knock on the front door surprised me. Looking out the window, I saw a uniformed stranger on the front porch. He knocked again.

I yelled through the door, "Can I help you? Are you looking for your pet?" He didn't answer, so I moved back toward the window to get a full view of him. He caught my movement, took a couple steps toward the window and launched himself through it, raining glass and himself down on me.

His weight was crushing me, and that was before he recovered from the intrusion. I pulled my right leg up and tried to hoist him off me and scoot out from under him. I elbowed him at his temple and kneed him in the balls. He responded with a random punch at my head that stunned me. It was a punch that meant business. He rolled away from me and jumped to his feet, holding his crotch area.

I stood and backed towards the curtains where I had placed a knife. Four feet separated us as we stared at each other.

"Why are you here? What do you want?"

He didn't answer. His response was to charge me like a football player. I lunged sideways. His half-hit was sufficient to knock me against the wall. I grabbed the curtain away from the wall and ripped my knife off the Velcro that held it. With a forceful shove, he spun me and pressed me against the wall, face first and was unaware of what I held.

He grabbed the back of my neck and breathed into it, then stood still, still pressing against me. Then his hand tugged at my waistband. He scraped my leggings down to my knees and pushed himself into the back of me. I froze. The scream was in my throat, and the urge to thrash around almost happened. My instincts surged as my primal brain took control.

I waited for him to pull his pants down as he grunted into my neck, informing me of his intentions. When I felt the pressure on my neck ease off, I pushed off from the wall and spun on him, slashing low as I turned. He didn't see my knife as I stabbed at his groin area, then sliced his wrist on the hand that still held his penis. He landed a left hook that knocked me sideways before it registered that he was bleeding profusely.

He looked down and made a blood curdling noise before he rushed me. I slashed wildly and pivoted away from him. He still had too much fight in him before he bled to death. I went for the door because I knew I could outrun him.

With his left hand, he grabbed my shirt from behind and pulled me to the floor on top of him. He wrapped his right arm that was spurting blood around my neck and hit me with his left. I angled my body out of the way as I plunged the knife into his thigh, near his groin, hoping to catch the femoral artery. His punches were still forceful enough to give me a skull fracture. Or break my hand that tried to protect my head before he died. His right arm went limp around my neck, but he kept hitting me with the left as I kept stabbing him. As fast and deep as I could muster.

Jeff's yelling brought me back from being unconscious. He hoisted me off the floor and carried me to the kitchen counter and sat me on it. He was still yelling and my head hurt like a hangover.

"Please, stop yelling."

He checked me all over to locate my injuries and the source of blood. Then he grabbed the kitchen rag and washed my face off with it. Once he was done with my top half, he noticed my pants were down. He grabbed my chin and asked me without asking me. I didn't want to cry in front of him, but I could barely say a word without my lips quivering and tears falling.

"He tried."

He helped me shimmy my pants up, then gave me a relieved hug.

"You're a fucking mess, you know that? God help us all."

He brought a chair in the kitchen and helped me sit in it, then handed me the rag to keep washing the blood off.

Jeff called his father to report an incident that needed to be cleaned up at the cabin. He quickly added that it wasn't me, but it was a terminal occurrence. He stood over the intruder, shaking his head after he hung up.

"We got our own Lizzy Borden right here. Holy shit, I mean."

He didn't know what to say. I got up to look at him and the blood made my wooziness worse. Jeff claimed the man's entire blood supply might be on the floor. I sat back down in the kitchen and didn't look anymore.

Jeff covered his face and exclaimed, "Joe is going to go ballistic over this. Damn it."

Then he grabbed his phone and took pictures of the guy and me. He used a rag to clean off a finger to send the print to Mickey for ID.

"I'm going to send these pictures to Mickey to show Joe. They probably need a brief explanation before he looks at them."

It wasn't his fault this guy came when he went to the store, but I knew he felt guilty. I knew Joe was going to lose his shit just like he said, too.

With a team of three in tow, JD entered to investigate while the others waited outside. Initially, he searched for me, then shifted focus to the man on the floor. "Christ."

Jeff had recovered from the shock of it and said, "Right?"

JD walked into the kitchen, dodging the blood and glass to get to me. After inspecting my head and face, he inquired about any other injuries. From the freezer, he grabbed a bag of frozen veggies and instructed me to apply it to my face.

He stood in front of me, shaking his head. "All this blood is his?"

I nodded yes and covered my face to hide the tears.

JD let in the three waiting men. They were wide eyed when they gingerly walked in. He told one to attend to me.

Jeff said, "I'd be careful if I were you."

JD gave him a dirty look. The guy had a medic bag with him and, after checking me out, declared I had a concussion with bruising and multiple abrasions from the window. He applied bandages and saved some for me to use later.

The two other guys worked the crime scene, taking pictures, measuring, and finally wrapping this guy up in a body bag. He quietly admitted to JD his lack of the ability to fix this. "We're going to have to outsource it."

JD replied, "You'll need to figure it out, no outsourcing. This is a confidential crime scene. Take care of it. You can take some plywood from the situation house to cover the window."

"Yes sir," was his answer as he helped carry the body bag out the door.

The medic returned with a tarp and covered the bloody area. "Just temporary. I think we'll need to replace the floor."

Fifteen minutes later, they were pounding nails into the window frame from the outside. Six MPs arrived to stand guard.

We stayed in the kitchen while they worked and waited until they left to talk about it. I washed off as best I could in the sink, then recounted what happened. I told them every detail, including what I was thinking when I did it. Jeff sat at the edge of his chair like he was ringside, but JD sat back, rigid, with his hands on his knees and a scowl on his face. They wondered who aided the guy's base entry without military affiliation, leaving them perplexed.

Several hours had passed since it happened, long enough for Joe to arrive in a helicopter, landing as close to the cabin as possible. Jeff and JD both tensed upon hearing the bird, but Jeff bravely opened the door to let him bypass the MPs.

His boots clunked on the porch stairs, followed by a brief pause before he entered. Joe caught sight of me and surveyed the room. He reached out for my hand, then picked me up and carried me upstairs gently.

He took my face in his enormous hands to look at me; I tried not to wince, but it hurt. He let go and started the shower for me.

"Let's get you cleaned up, ok?"

Joe got in the shower with me and washed me from head to toe. I had tiny cuts from rolling on the glass and a long scratch when he tried pulling my pants. The scratch burned when he went over it with soap. He touched my shoulder as if to ask. I gave him the fifty-cent version of what happened, and he was content with that.

He dried me, dressed me and put me to bed. "I'll get you some pain meds."

I shook my head no. "The medic diagnosed me with a concussion. Should I take any medication?"

The muscles in his jaw tightened before he said he'd be right back.

A few minutes later, he slipped into bed and woke me every hour to check on me and tell me he loved me.

DAY NINETEEN

I woke up feeling like I had never gone to sleep. I slithered out of bed. My head felt fuzzy and distorted, and I realized why upon seeing my reflection. My face was dark and swollen, my left eye was bloodshot, my neck was red and blue, and parts of my skull had knots on it. What a sight. I got dressed and slowly went downstairs.

Joe greeted me and guided me to a barstool in the kitchen. Eddie, Alex, Bobby and Jeff stood there staring at me like a zoo animal. Alex took a step toward me and I put my hand up to stop him.

"Don't touch me. I know you want to, but it all hurts."

He said, "I'll just get a closer look." With a small penlight, he checked my eyes and examined my scalp.

Joe served me a cup of coffee and Eddie asked what he could cook me for breakfast.

"Bacon."

He winked. "That's always the answer."

Jeff was leaning against the counter, looking at me. He rubbed his face and said, "If you couldn't take care of yourself, you'd be dead. So, good job."

Joe put his head down, and I knew he was trying not to explode.

I touched his arm and said, "It's not his fault and it's never going to be anyone's fault if they kill me. No matter where I am. I've been alone on base plenty of times because it's our safe space. You're not supposed to have to babysit me here. All of this is Michael's fault. It's his fault and I'm glad I killed him and the rest of them for what they did to me and my friends. I accept the consequences and apologize for everyone having to do the same."

Bobby was so thoughtful when he said, "We're all in this with you. There's no separation. You're a sister in arms and family. We'll always have your back. Anytime, anywhere. Period. But like Jeff said, it's good you can handle yourself."

Eddie placed a pile of bacon in front of me while he continued cooking more bacon and eggs. I nibbled on them while they tried to revise their plan for here and Binghamton.

Eddie rummaged in a drawer when he got ready to butter the toast. "The knives have once again spread throughout the house, haven't they? Guess that's a good thing."

Joe left the room after receiving a call from his father. When he returned, he announced the base was on lockdown and we needed to choose where I would live for the next month. My options were South Dakota, Montana, or Wyoming.

I turned to look at him so fast I got dizzy. "What the hell? Now I'm being exiled? And to some state where it's still cold? Why those states?"

Jeff said, "They're predominately conservative states with little known radical groups or antigovernment groups."

Joe added, "Eddie's going with you."

Eddie whipped around to face him. "I vote for Wyoming. Best place to go hunting." He waited for me to agree, and Joe sent his father a text with our wishes.

Alex offered me a pillow case with soft ice packs in with some ace wrap. "May I?"

I shivered and said, "Just go really easy." He carefully wrapped my head up and said, "We'll take it off in thirty minutes."

Eddie plated breakfast for everyone and we ate in silence until Jeff started laughing like he was insane.

Bobby asked, "Are you having a delayed reaction to last night's events?" I just thought he was nuts. He kept laughing, shaking his head and rubbing his face.

I asked, "What the hell is wrong with you?"

He stopped laughing. "Last night you went all Jack the Ripper on a guy twice your size, slaughtered a house full of bad guys without weapons, you've been shot and beat up and you're just sitting there eating your bacon like it's all in a day's work. You're either a psychopath or you're so much like your father, it's the best gift in the world. Either way, some enlisted men haven't seen as much action as you."

Joe couldn't hold back. "It's a damn good thing she's like him or she'd be dead this morning."

Jeff agreed. "You can blame me. I left her here alone."

I stopped them by saying, "I've been here plenty of times alone. You can't protect every minute. We already had this conversation. Now drop it."

I took the ice packs off my head and went upstairs with Joe. We lie facing each other on the bed. He expressed his intention to go back there tomorrow.

"The most random people are involved. They can't explain why or even identify whom they got involved with. They took bribes or favors, ultimately just being about money, not ideology. Until we get them all, it's not over. It'll take as long as it takes. And the brother of your guy, we've not connected him to anything yet."

Joe was casually running his hands over my arms and back, my hands on his chest, then lower. He didn't feel so casual down there.

"Rae, I don't think your head can take it. We shouldn't."

I needed to connect with him, so I undressed and waited for him to follow suit.

"Just go slow."

We had the best, slowest, hardly moving sex that we've ever had. My head felt like it was going to explode, but it was worth it. He covered me up and left the bedroom.

After a few hours of sleep, I glided downstairs. The guys were watching the crew clean the bloodstain from the wood floor. They were collecting glass from ten feet away. Upon moving a chair, they noticed a chunk of flesh underneath. The gloved crew member picked it up and almost dropped it.

He opened his hand to show the guys and said, "I believe it's the tip of his penis."

They all squirmed and touched their crotches.

Behind them, I cleared my throat. "Guess he didn't see the sign about what happens to intruders."

Joe met me at the bottom step and whispered, "I'm so proud of you."

The crew averted their gazes from the monster I was and kept working.

"Let's get out of their way. We've got to get some things organized for your trip to Wyoming," said Joe.

Jeff volunteered to stay behind to watch the crew.

Eddie seemed excited. "It's considered normal to possess multiple guns in Wyoming. Hunters go there all the time. And I believe we have some brothers up there to call on if needed." He looked at Joe and said, "I'll get our weapons ready. I know what ones she can handle."

Alex said, "I wonder how many first-aid kits we can fit in here?"

I punched him in the arm and he gave me a side hug.

The general rang Joe again, telling him he recalled everyone that was on base yesterday, and they would be here in two hours. He gave permission for any interrogation methods necessary to find out who was involved.

"You really think you'll be able to figure it out?" I asked skeptically.

Joe stated he got on base with authorized help. "Through conducting background checks on everyone present, we identified about a dozen individuals with suspicious data."

I understood that to mean Mickey had tapped into their phones to determine that information.

We milled around outside until the cleaning crew came outside and started on the window. FETCH couldn't just watch. They all lent a hand to finish the job. It took their brute strength to lift the bullet proof glass into place. That should keep the riff-raff from crashing through it. The crew said they ordered new windows for the entire cabin. I didn't mind the overkill.

JD arrived in uniform and told us to be at the box, dressed in our FETCH uniforms in ten minutes. He glanced at me and said, "You, too."

We changed, adorned ourselves with weapons and drove to the box instead of walking. There were six MPs checking everyone in, telling them where to stand. JD motioned for us to stand in front of them. Everyone's attention was on me and my battered head. MPs distributed papers to both sides of the group and instructed them to pass them around. They looked disgusted and looked at me after they passed it.

Leaning in, Bobby whispered, "The guy from last night." I couldn't believe JD would do that.

JD addressed the men. "Our country must combat numerous challenges, but our sworn soldiers should not be among them. Traitors. And today, we are standing amongst them, one at least, maybe more." He walked back and forth, making eye contact with them. "It would expedite the process of court martial if the parties responsible for the attack on Mrs. Cokely last night came forward. We'll stay until we discover who aided the civilian and orchestrated the assault on the innocent woman."

Joe jumped from the front to the back line to punch a guy so hard he fell back unconscious. Bobby held me in place by touching my arm and shaking his head.

Joe walked to the front of the group and said, "Anyone else think that's funny? That my wife isn't innocent? You come through me next time. Let me set the story straight. Her husband bilked an anti-government group out of millions. Not her. This terrorist group killed her friends, one by one, at a dinner party. She fought to survive. Just like we all have. She is not the enemy. Killing her won't stop the quest to find them all. It would only fuel the fight."

JD told everyone to remain standing and he would start the interviews. He directed the first soldier to move forward and interrogated him in front of the entire group. At around the seventh soldier, one guy lied and was promptly called out by another soldier.

"You weren't there, man. What are you talking about?"

Further discussion revealed he's a cheater, not a terrorist. After he questioned all of them, he called ten of them up front and asked them more pointed questions about their beliefs and history of being in the military. The innocent ones looked pissed that their loyalty was in question. The two guilty ones looked scared. That was my take.

Jeff showed up and handed me the knife I used last night. "Got it all cleaned up for you."

He said it louder than needed and smiled at the men in question. The two nervous guys looked at FETCH, the general, the MPs, and kept shifting their weight and their eyes. JD kept asking questions, excusing the others until he got to the two on the end. The others recognized some shit was about to happen. JD stepped back until he was in line with us.

We observed the two men who didn't proclaim innocence and appeared to accept their fate. They both looked at me with contempt.

I finally had to ask. "What did I do to deserve your hatred? Do you even know my story? My history? What will my death accomplish?"

One of them said, "You aren't even military, and you got an entire squad trying to avenge your situation. What has it done for me? Send me away for so long my wife left me. I don't even know my kids anymore. And for what? This fucked up country that doesn't give a shit about it's military? Only to see it throw all kinds of resources at you."

Someone in the group yelled, "Your wife left because you're an asshole!"

Several murmured agreements. FETCH remained quiet and let the tension build.

I decided to test the folklore of my dad's name and stepped forward to say, "My father was Roly Sampson. Perhaps you've heard of him. His reputation has afforded me the honor of belonging to FETCH." Recognition drifted across their faces, like the last piece of the puzzle just landed. "I'll tell you this, so you can tell others when my name comes up. I survived four men that were after something my husband took from them. It wasn't me or anyone else they killed.

Senseless killing. We were all innocent, but I was the lone survivor of that weekend."

I made eye contact with as many as possible, hoping to humanize myself. "I've tried to separate myself and escape from the past. But the radicals came after me again. What was I to do? Give up?" The group yelled support their respective chants.

JD stepped forward. "I'm going to initiate your court martial for treason. You'll have the rest of your lives to think about it."

The asshole said, "Just shoot me now."

The other guy fell to his knees and asked for leniency. They were both loudly belittled by their fellow soldiers. JD nodded to the MPs, and they took the two into custody.

JD dismissed the group and left. Several guys came forward and told Joe that they've made applications to join FETCH. They assured him in the meantime he'd have their support and asked what skills to improve to advance their chances of being chosen. Eddie motioned for me to join him, and we walked to the shooting range.

"I've picked out our weapons and want you to fire them all at least once. Even the big ones."

I laughed. "Even the big ones, huh? I know some names and numbers of them."

He looked skeptical. "We'll see."

We began with pistols, but the noise, even with protection, was too loud. "Eddie, this is killing my head. We'll have to practice when we get there." Initially disappointed, he then examined my head and bumps closely.

"Jesus, you are a mess. I guess you're good enough until we get there."

I scoffed, "Good enough? I'm a damn good shot." We gathered our guns and ammo and called Bobby for a ride back to the cabin.

The cabin had a new window; the blood was gone and the chemical smell hung thick in the air. "Guess I'll go get packed. And I'm bringing two suitcases for all my warm clothes."

Eddie said, "It's starting to warm up. You'll be alright."

Joe came upstairs while I was packing to say goodbye. "We've got to head back. You know I hate leaving you, right?"

I hugged him around the waist and said, "Of course I know. I hate it, but I know."

He sat on the bed, and I straddled him for some soft farewell kisses.

Joe said, "I need you to."

I stopped him and said, "I know everything you're going to say. I already know, ok? We'll both be alright, and when we reunite, they'll be less bad guys out there."

He hugged me tight, kissed me hard on the lips, stood and walked out the door.

I stayed upstairs packing and didn't start crying until I heard the chopper take off. I fight with the devil and angel on my shoulders, keep fighting, or slink off into oblivion. Each day, I weigh the options: risking my life or living safely in another country, alone. After I get over the self-pity, I always choose Joe. And that means fighting.

Eddie knocked and pushed the door open to check my progress on packing. "Make sure you bring those heavy socks. Jeff's still here. He made some questionable slop for dinner. It smells good, though."

I tossed more socks in my bag. "Wow, that was really enticing. I'll race you to the table."

The slop was like hamburger helper without the box, and it tasted pretty good. They were both getting constant texts and telling me the important stuff. Eddie was grateful to Mickey for securing the hunting passes and explaining the difficulty of getting them on short notice. For Jeff, it was that he and his father finalized his team roster.

He added, "We took the ones you guys picked out and narrowed it down, all with Joe's blessing. Don't worry."

My head still hurts. I cleared my plate and went to bed.

DAY TWENTY

Jeff and Eddie were making breakfast when I went downstairs. It seems all we ever do is eat, but they're all huge guys and need to maintain their strength. I need to as well. Jeff put a folder in front of me with our IDs, passports, personal information that we needed to remember for our little stint in Wyoming. Eddie couldn't use his real name for fear they'd tie him to me. Eddie was the new Freddie, and I was Rayne.

They carried my suitcases to the truck, and we were on the road by eight.

"It's about 2,000 miles to Dubois, so get comfy." Eddie didn't have to tell me twice. I reclined the seat and fell asleep.

He nudged me awake in Tennessee when we stopped for gas. I put my gloves and hat on to avoid any tattoo recognition cameras when I went to the bathroom. Loaded with an arm full of drinks and snacks, we continued our journey. He handed me an energy drink and a bag of Fritos.

"Do you want me to drive?" He raised his eyebrows and shook his head no. We ate our snacks as loud as we could and laughed like kids.

"Eddie, I mean, Freddie, we've been on our own before. I'll take your lead, don't worry. I trust you, and I want to say this up front. If something happens to me, it's not your fault.

I mean that. I told Joe that too. So, thank you for putting your neck on the line for me."

"Jesus, stop being so morbid." He turned the radio down. "Nobody's going to die. We're going to go hunting and fishing and make fires to keep your delicate ass warm and drink beer and eat what we kill. That's the extent of it."

I looked at him and said, "What we kill? I'm not killing anything except a fish. But I'll eat what you kill."

We shook on it and rocked out until we reached our target hotel.

We ordered room service and fell asleep watching Taken on TV.

DAY TWENTY-ONE

"You snore like a dang bear. Never heard you before."

My head still hurts. "I slept in a funny position trying to avoid pressure on my swollen spots. My neck is killing me now, too." He was ready and dressed to go.

"Get moving, we've got to hit the road in 20." I rolled out of bed, took a quick shower and was ready with a minute to spare.

We drove a few hours before we got breakfast at a drive thru. "It'll be dark when we reach our destination, as this leg takes around 14 hours. I hate to miss the scenery going in."

I asked, "Have you been here before?"

He smiled, "We trained out here, in Yellowstone and the surrounding states. You get a vast variety of terrain and weather to prepare you for anywhere." He stared forward like he was deep in thought. "Quite a few guys retire in these places. Sparse population, the wilderness, freedom, but mostly less bullshit to deal with. Solitude is sometimes the best remedy for PTSD. It's hard for some vets to relax in public, to transition back to civilian life. Sometimes you just can't un-flip that switch."

It made me sad listening to him, but I knew even I wasn't the same after my initial incident. Accumulated stress becomes ingrained in your being.

"Do you think about retiring? Getting married? Kids? Any of that?"

He kind of squinted and half smiled. "I think about all of that, Rae. Don't know if I'll ever be ready for it. Besides, being in FETCH doesn't really afford that lifestyle."

I laughed. "You mean the chances of you finding someone as fucked up as me to join our team are slim to none? Joe's the only lucky one?" We shared a sad, knowing look.

After a few hours, we paused, refueled, relieved ourselves, and took a brief walk. Nobody paid attention to us, not even a glance our way.

"We'll need to stop for gas one more time before we get to our cabin."

I whirled around and asked, "Cabin? What do you mean cabin? I hope that place has both heat and running water."

He rolled his eyes. "Of course it does. You'll love it."

"It's really dark out here. You sure the GPS is right?"

With a smile, he suggested, "Just look at the sky. We're almost there."

"You said that 20 minutes ago, when we drove through the city."

I pushed my face forward, almost touching the windshield, and was in awe of the countless stars and moody color of the sky. We turned on an unpaved road and drove up an incline. Our cabin was at least a football field off the road.

"How can there be power out here?" I tried not to panic. He ignored me.

He left the truck lights shining as we got our gear and hauled it up on the covered porch. Stacks of wood sat at both ends of the porch. He lifted the mat and got the key to enter, gun in hand. Using a flashlight, he found a table lamp near the door. It was a pleasant surprise to discover the heat was on. "I can't believe they have power out here."

Eddie brought all the bags in and we got settled quickly.

"I'm going to make a fire." He declared. "How about you heat some soup from the supply bag? We'll make a grocery run in the morning."

We ate our Progresso soup and fell asleep in front of the fire.

DAY TWENTY-TWO

It was still dark when Eddie kicked me awake. He shook me, put a gun in my hand and told me to follow him. Then I heard it. Scraping noises on the porch. We crept to the window to peek outside. His shoulders dropped, and he pulled me forward to look.

There were two deer or elk rubbing their antlers on the porch posts. "They should have gotten rid of them by now. Probably young."

Tiptoeing to the door, he suggested, "Let's get a closer look."

We put our coats on and slowly opened the door. Two steps out and they saw us. They jumped so high it made me jump and fall back. They bounded away, sounding like they weighed a ton on the cold, hard ground.

"Well, that was exciting. Can we add more logs to the fire? It makes it seem so much warmer than the heat." I meant for him to do it. I curled up on the couch, waiting for the warmth to reach me. "Were you awake or did that wake you up?"

Eddie said, "It woke me up."

He was in soldier mode, and he was one of the best. I fell back asleep and woke to the sun coming in the windows.

My feet were warm when I walked to the bathroom. Eddie said they had radiant heat in the floors.

"Once we've finished placing the cameras, we can go into town to get groceries."

I looked at myself in the bathroom mirror and groaned. My head shape was back to normal, but the bruising looked green today. What a sight. I grabbed a wig with long hair and put a hat on over it. That should disguise it enough.

The ride back to town was spectacular. Cold weather aside, living here would be perfect. And well, except for the wildlife, too. Not a fan of bears.

Eddie pushed the cart that was full of canned goods and boxes of carbs.

"The fewer trips to town, the better."

The whole cart said unhealthy to me.

A concerned older woman looked me over intently and whispered, making sure I was okay.

I nodded and said, "I am now. He's my brother. Thanks."

Her sweetness surprised me and tears welled. Guess I didn't hide my bruising enough to fool anyone. Eddie paid cash, and we loaded the truck on a now very windy, sunny day. So windy it blew my hat off, and I thought my wig too. I tried to catch my hat and hold my wig down, just as a pickup pulled into the spot next to us.

As the man from the pickup truck stepped out, my bruised face became even more visible by my hair blowing straight back.

He looked at me, then Eddie, and balled his fists. "Are you ok, Miss? Did he do that to you?"

Eddie backed up and said, "Whoa, dude, that's my sister. I removed her from the situation that caused it."

I pointed to my face. "He didn't do this. As the saying goes, you should see the other guy." I neglected to tell him he was missing his penis.

Eddie shook his head and laughed. He extended his hand and said, "Freddie, nice to meet you. Thanks for looking out. This is my sister, Rayne."

He said his name was Wayne. He was probably in his 50s, almost as tall as Eddie and at least forty pounds heavier. Eddie noticed an Airforce tattoo on his forearm and asked about it. The guy didn't seem convinced about our story and told Eddie that they keep track of the folks that come to town and weed out the undesirables.

As we drove home, he handed me his phone and told me to text Mickey and ask him to find information about our new friend. "Never know who'll come in handy. His genuine concern for your face is a promising sign toward an excellent ally."

We left groceries on the counter for Eddie to organize based on our meals and restocking needs. "Now we just need a protein source."

I looked at him funny.

"Kill something to eat is what I'm saying. You've had deer before, right?"

I shook my head yes. "Not for a long time, but I'll definitely eat it."

Eddie pulled out two vests for our walk to familiarize ourselves with the area around the cabin.

"What is all this stuff?"

He pulled everything out of the compartments, one by one, and told me. "Bear spray, skunk scent, knife, stop bleed, gauze wrap, tactical baton, two flashbangs and extra ammo. Should be all we need."

It worried me that we needed all that just to go for a walk. He handed me a rifle, and I holstered my pistol.

It was sunny but chilly. The air quality was like I've never breathed before. Eddie was sucking it all in.

"You smell that?" I shook my head no and took a few more big whiffs. He said, "Exactly, there is no smell. Just air. Crisp, clean air. Now, let's double time it."

He took off at a small jog, which meant a fast jog for my shorter legs.

On a hill, he suddenly halted and signaled for me to stop. We squatted down and watched a group of bison about 100 yards away. "Wow, those things are huge. Even from here. What the hell are those tourists thinking when they get so close?"

Eddie shook his head and said, "One of them would feed us for months." That was a red flag.

"Months? Wasn't it only supposed to last a month? Why did you say months?"

He kept watching the bison and said, "I was just making a statement about how big they are. Have you ever had bison meat? It's stronger than beef, but when you cook it right, it's pretty good, especially burgers."

We waited for the big cows to mosey away before we walked the ridge of the hill, followed by marching the perimeter of our cabin for miles around. Identifying poop piles is a useful and potentially life-saving skill, he said.

Eddie placed colored markers in different locations after he sighted them in for distances of 100 yards. He explained it was leg work to measure the distance in case he was in a hurry. He was being his own scout.

"Terrain like this makes judging distance challenging. You'll find shooting easier, and I'll dial it in quicker."

We trekked up and down the hills until we got back to where we started, and completed a dang marathon run in four hours.

"After all that work, I'm excited to open a can of Beenie weenies." I was sarcastic and disappointed.

We had been there less than 24 hours and I was already fidgety. "Eddie, Freddie, what's the plan for the next month?"

He sat back and said, "Number one, stay alive. Number two, hunt. Three, train. Four, go through files of applicants for other teams. Five, be ready for whatever happens. No worries about roadside bombs here. Consider that a big plus."

I immediately regretted complaining. "If you ever want to discuss that, I'm here to listen."

He cocked his head thoughtfully. "Thanks, but you've seen enough shit. No need to burden you with more."

His phone rang with a number he didn't recognize. He answered it but said nothing. His face transformed from confusion to anger. I got off the sofa and stood next to him, hoping to hear the conversation from a voice I didn't recognize. Eddie repeated coordinates that meant nothing to me and said, "Exfil, 2100, copy."

He hung up and texted Mickey. "Are you aware?" He texted back, "Copy, 2100. Air support questionable."

Eddie flung his phone down on the couch and said, "Pack it up, we're getting out of dodge, asap."

He packed all the guns and ammo first, followed by his personal items, and then some groceries. After packing and getting ready, I looked out the front window aimlessly. He wouldn't answer any of my questions while he was packing.

"Do you have everything? We won't be coming back." I nodded yes.

"You drive." He got in the back seat and laid his guns out with extra ammo at his feet.

"Tell me what happened. Now, Eddie."

"It seems we have a target on our back already. Four guys were overheard talking about a vulnerable female that was in town this morning. The kind that might pay to keep her location hidden. That guy we met, Wayne, overheard them and could only guess it was you. He made calls until he reached the right people. He had no other knowledge and lost sight of them after the diner."

I pounded the steering wheel. "I thought this place was safe? Did we actually drive to Wyoming for only one day of peace? I can't believe it. Can't I go anywhere?"

Eddie calmly informed me they might not know my identity. "Just opportunists wanting to get rich off domestic violence. Sounds unrelated to me, and now is not the time for self-pity, Rachel. Buck up and stay in the moment."

I held my piss-off comment and drove.

I drove east with the shine from a half-moon, and the wind blowing us into the other lane. "Is someone picking us up or what are we doing? They can't send a chopper in this wind, can they?"

Eddie said, "It's another cabin, about 30 minutes away. And no, they can't send a chopper in the wind."

I kept getting madder the more I drove.

"Let's go back. We can hide on the hill and shoot whoever comes to the cabin. Especially if you don't think they're professionals. We can do it. I can help you."

Minutes passed before he broke his silence with a command. "Pull over."

After I did, he stated, "My responsibility is to keep you safe, not engage in any unnecessary gunfights. I trust you to do as I say. I can handle the rest. Turn it around and we'll take care of them." I saluted him as I spun the truck around and gunned it.

We parked off-road, concealed in bushes, a hundred yards from our cabin's driveway. We then trekked the hillside until spotting the cabin.

I told Eddie, "I don't think I've ever been this scared before. I keep thinking about all the wildlife out here. They're probably hunting us, too."

He snapped at me, "Focus on the cabin. Keep sweeping the area with your scope. And remember, I can outrun you."

I kicked him and said, "You ass."

On the main highway, we spotted three sets of lights in the distance. The first set drove by, the second two disappeared.

"Train your sight on the driveway." Two trucks with their lights off crept up the long dirt road. Four individuals exited two trucks, which halted about fifty feet from the cabin. Through my scope, I saw they were carrying long guns.

Eddie said, "Don't shoot, keep your focus on the last guy."

We watched as they approached the cabin and circled it, trying to see inside. Three of them returned to the front, while one stayed behind the house.

Eddie said, "Stay focused on the porch. There's going to be a kaboom."

After eliminating the man behind the house, he fired into the cabin. Before they could get off the porch to run to their buddy, the house exploded in spectacular fashion. I screamed in surprise.

"I told you we weren't going back. I loosened up the gas line before we left."

We sat back and watched the cabin burn. Eddie lamented, "I feel bad about polluting this area with the cabin fire."

After a few minutes, I asked, "What's our move? Call the police? Hide them? What about their trucks?"

He grabbed up his equipment and said, "Come on, I don't want to meet law enforcement yet. Who knows how their emergency response system works out here? But just in case, let's get their trucks out of sight."

I was sure I'd die before we got off the hill, trying to keep up, looking for bear and carrying my rifle.

One truck had the keys in it, so we used it to push the other sideways off the road and, luckily, down a steep embankment. Next, we drove their truck to where we parked our truck up the road, drove their truck off into the woods, and switched vehicles.

Eddie took a different route than the one Mickey specified for the cabin. "We need cover and we need guys like Wayne. Our best option is to hang out in town and have them watch out for us. We can say your ex is hunting for you. If we can get Wayne to sell that idea with his friends, we should be ok."

It sounded reasonable to me. He handed me his phone, and I sent Mickey a text with our new plan. He responded a few minutes later. "Wayne will meet you at the diner. All set."

We sat outside and waited for Wayne to show. He had two other guys in his pickup. He motioned for us to follow him further down the road to a closed office building parking lot. They got out, then Eddie did. After a brief conversation, Eddie opened my door. Wayne introduced me to his buddies who were also ex-military. One of them served under General Cokely and vaguely remembered his kids. Eddie gave them the cliff notes history of FETCH and why we're here. They pledged support, and we followed them back to Wayne's house, about ten minutes from town.

Wayne invited the guys to come back in the morning for follow-up plans. He showed us his rustic house and where we could sleep tonight.

"We'll figure something else out tomorrow, ok?"

Eddie thanked him and said, "No problem, that couch looks comfortable, by my standards. Rae, you got the bedroom."

Eddie stored our gear in my room and blocked the window with a dresser. "Shoot first, ask questions later. Night."

I kept my clothes on under the covers and fell fast asleep.

DAY TWENTY-THREE

I threw the covers off when I heard Eddie and Wayne talking. It took me a minute to adjust to my surroundings. A sparse room with a wooden bed, dresser, and nightstand - aged yet tidy. The walls were bare, and the paint was dull. Wayne either didn't care or liked the 1950s ambiance.

I joined them in the living room. Wayne pointed to the kitchen where the coffee was. As I filled my cup, he apologized for having to drink it black. I sipped the black lava and thanked him, anyway. It made me shudder.

During our conversation, he mentioned he spends a majority of his time outdoors, even in winter, and owns two additional properties in Wyoming. He told us where they were, in case we needed another place to go.

Andy and Ritt from last night arrived at 8am. They both had their own coffee.

Ritt said, "Should've thought to bring you some coffee. His stuff will kill ya. Or make you shit your pants." He lowered his head, embarrassed by what he said.

Eddie was quick to speak up. "You can't offend this one with language, or talk about bowel movements. She's unfazed by any of that. But thanks for thinking she was."

I smiled as I put down my coffee. "Well, perhaps we could go into town for breakfast." I said, as hopeful and polite as I could. I didn't want to offend our new friends.

The men stood at the diner's door, trying to figure out their seating arrangement. None of them desired to sit with their back against the door. We moved to the diner's rear and set up a table for everyone to face sideways. I guess we all have issues.

Ritt and Eddie monopolized the conversation around hunting. When I finished eating, I threw a dig at them.

"To me, it's really not fair that a sniper hunts with a rifle. You should use a bow, or a pistol. I mean, can they even smell you a mile away?"

With heads tucked and eyebrows raised, they exchanged looks.

Andy bluntly stated, "I'm not getting close to a bear, that's for sure. Or anything else that can kill me. I'm getting out of the woods and putting meat on the table the safest way I can."

I thought about it and said, "I see your point."

Andy added, "And not everyone can shoot from a mile away."

With a raised eyebrow, he turned to Eddie, sparking a conversation about Eddie's confirmed kills.

Eddie wiped his mouth off before disclosing, "Accurate to around 3500 yards. The sweet spot is less, of course."

He shook his head and said, "Rae was on a boat with her uncle, who was about to shoot her and I missed the kill shot. My biggest failure to date."

I was quick to point out, "I was moving all around. It was dark and the waves were throwing us around. It was my fault. I got in the way." He was irritated and looked away.

Wayne asked, "So what happened?"

I told them, "He hit him in the chest or shoulder. It knocked him into the water, but he shot through the boat and hit me in the stomach. We never found his body. Should you encounter a man with a charred face in town, kill him. Quick."

Ritt said, "I think we should finish this conversation outside."

While driving to Wayne's place, Eddie suggested recruiting guys for a local team. "These three individuals are potential backup team members. If something happens nearby, we can count on them, even if not regularly."

He handed me his phone. "Send their names to Mickey and let's get them checked out." We were only back at Wayne's ten minutes before Mickey wrote back A+.

Eddie elaborated on FETCH's functions and inquired about potential affiliation. Andy questioned whether we were a covert organization resembling the CIA, and stated that he wouldn't be interested if we were. After sizing me up, he questioned my military affiliation.

"I wasn't in the military."

Ritt asked, "Can you tell us how you're involved, then? I like to know the characters I associate with."

My secrets weren't really secret anymore, so I gave them my version of it. "I was the only survivor of a radical, home-grown terrorist group that staged a home invasion. My husband at the time stole millions of dollars from their group. Unfortunately, they believe I was part of it and are still searching to recover the money. They use ransom money from the rich and famous to fund themselves. We train those people who may become targets, and those who've already had threats to survive an attack." They all looked like they had more questions, the more I talked.

"Why did you survive?" Ritt asked, leaning forward in his chair.

Standing by the fireplace, I turned to face them as I spoke. "There were four of them and eight of us. They killed six of us. I killed five, including my husband, who was trying to kill me so he could live and join them. My father taught me survival skills, and I guess my instincts took over."

Wayne said, "Mighty good instincts."

Andy inquired, "What's the procedure for joining FETCH? I'm in."

Eddie smiled as the other two agreed. "We have well-rounded teams, each person with a specialty. Sniper, bomb, weapons, medical, flight. We'd like to add a few more guys to this area. Any suggestions?"

Wayne stated the need for collective brainstorming to identify capable candidates. "I'm familiar with a few guys that qualify, but mentally, I wouldn't give them 100%."

Eddie was quick to say, "They have to be 100 percent solid. And we dive deep into them. So only the best. FETCH is the new special-special forces. Even though you'll be home based, we need the best when we need it."

Wayne looked at his watch. "Let's go to the ranch. It's an hour from here. We can show our skills out there."

"This state doesn't get enough attention for its beauty." Eddie was intent on the drive while my head swiveled at the scenery. "How old do you think they are? Fifties?"

He said, "Ask Mickey. And ask about Wayne's property holdings. Also, get a list of retired veterans nearby."

The further we drove, the fewer cars we saw. Wayne turned off a dirt road and drove another mile before we saw an expansive house.

I looked at Eddie. "How is this possible?"

He laughed and said, "If the guy was in-country, he got extra pay and nowhere to spend it. A lot of lifers have a million or so in pay they never spent. Guess Wayne was good with his money."

As I opened the truck door, the wind snatched it away. I jumped out and shoved it closed. Eddie shouldered a rifle and instructed me to have access to my weapon. "Open your coat."

Through my teeth I said, "What the hell? What are you thinking?"

He said, "Always be ready in an unfamiliar environment." Then he stood looking all around the property, telling Wayne he was loving the sights.

Wayne yelled over his shoulder as he opened the front door, "Come on in." Andy and Ritt arrived at the same time we reached the door.

This log cabin ranch was an open concept and high ceilings. Despite its appearance, the building was actually a single story, not two. He gave us a tour, four massive bedrooms, an office, a workout room, a gun room with a table to work on them, and the gigantic kitchen. He didn't mention another room at the end of the hall. No dining room or table, just a massive island. I complemented him on all his décor choices.

He laughed. "I bought it this way, mostly. Had to change a few things. I do appreciate the jacuzzi outside though. Helps the old bones."

"I've got some targets outside. We can fire some off. Haven't tested out in a while. I only shoot for food now."

Eddie said, "No problem, that's a real welcome change."

We walked outside and Ritt and Andy both had rifles on their shoulders and carried a box of ammo. We walked to our truck, got my rifle, and headed towards a spot where he had made a long table out of a tree. You could prop your guns and set your ammo down on it. Eddie stood back and watched the others get ready to shoot. He nodded for me to get into position.

The targets were a helluva distance away. They shot in order, left to right, each hitting the target. I took my shot and miraculously hit my target, too. I wanted to jump and dance, but pretended it was normal. Eddie looked proud. He probably held his breath while I took aim. They shot a few more times, each doing well, getting compliments from Eddie.

He asked, "Close range? Pistols?"

Wayne pointed. "Over this way." They left their rifles on the tree table and walked behind a shed.

Andy asked as we got set up to shoot, "So, your father was in, but you weren't?"

I didn't even glance at him when I said, "My dad was killed when I was 16. I was completely unaware of his job in the military."

They looked confused by my answer. I was really uncomfortable telling these strangers all my secrets so soon.

Eddie volunteered, "You may have heard of her dad, Roly Sampson?"

Ritt immediately said, "Are you shitting me? He was a fucking legend. I still want to believe he's hiding out somewhere."

Damn, that sentiment got stuck in my throat. I croaked out a thanks and loaded my pistol.

Ritt said, "I'm all in for FETCH. Check out anything you need."

We stayed outside shooting for another hour before Wayne suggested we walk the grounds. "I want to show you some safeguards I have. I'm actually trying to patent some of my designs. Chances are they'd be helpful to your clients."

First, he showed us a greenhouse that looked dilapidated.

"The top is actually solar panels to power underneath. The condensation build-up and rain catcher on the outside supply your water. You can control the airflow internally and externally by opening or closing the pipes, which also feature internal filtration."

Me and Eddie eyeballed each other like holy shit. This guy is brilliant. Wayne opened the door and inside looked as un-cared for as outside. He shifted objects to uncover a trapdoor to a cement room. We climbed down the ladder stairs and stood in a small room. We watched him move garden tools around to reveal a door to a larger room.

"This 10 x 10 room is steel framed and cement cased. It has drainage and vents to outside, controlled in here. Enough food and water for six months, and batteries to last a year. I've got one tunnel complete, two in progress, and I've almost perfected the periscope." He was proud, as he should be.

Eddie said, "This is genius. You should definitely market it. We'll help sell it for you."

Andy and Ritt said their goodbyes late afternoon and Eddie said we'd be in touch. Wayne asked Eddie if he wanted to hunt dinner and he eagerly accepted.

"Ok if I stay here?"

Eddie nearly declined, but Wayne unveiled a safe room in the house.

Two hours later, they drug an enormous deer up the driveway and over to a tree with a winch attached. They dressed it out and brought pieces of it into the house for me to cook. I fried up the loins with garlic, onions, and spices.

Wayne remarked on the lack of female cooking in his house after entering. "Smells delicious."

I asked him about it.

"The military got the best of me. What remains isn't husband material."

I scoffed. "You simply haven't met her yet. Look at me. I used to think the same thing, then I met Joe."

After dinner, Eddie was busy looking at the files Mickey sent him and asked Wayne if he had additional facts that weren't in the reports. Wayne ruled out three guys as soon as he heard their names.

"I don't trust them. Can't tell you why, but I don't."

Eddie crossed them off at his word. Five other guys stood out and we asked Mickey to dig deeper.

Wayne noted the time and pulled his coat on. "We need to clean up the deer pile better. Don't need any predators coming around tonight."

They grabbed freezer bags and garbage bags on the way outside. I cleaned up the kitchen and retired to bed while they were still outside.

Eddie knocked and came into my bedroom later. He sat on my bed and inquired, "Are you comfortable with the safe room? How about the greenhouse?"

I patted his hand and said I was. "You've got my permission to go hunting until your heart's content."

He punched me in the shoulder. "Night."

DAY TWENTY-FOUR

I snuggled under the comforter when I woke up. I missed Joe, and I wasn't eager to start another day here having to hide. All the talk about my dad yesterday had me melancholy and angry. Who was I now? I wouldn't think twice about shooting a person coming for me, but I didn't want to kill an animal that would feed me. Except for a bear, I'd shoot one of those in a heartbeat. They scare me like swamps do. I tossed the covers off, scampered to the bathroom, got dressed, and joined Eddie and Wayne.

"We contacted two of the guys. We're going to meet them in town. I don't like everyone knowing about this place." Wayne said as he sipped his black lava.

Eddie said, "You can stay here, but stay inside, ok?" He winked, "I'll bring you back some creamer."

Before they left, Wayne turned his computer on and gave the password in case it timed out.

I walked around the house, looked out every window, opened every drawer in public space, and lifted a few knives to stow in strategic spots. I pushed on the furniture to gage which pieces I could move quickly to bar a door and loosened the lamp shades in case I needed the metal U shape holders for weapons as a last resort. There were enough deer antlers hanging on the walls to gouge somebody's eyes out or do soft tissue damage. I got my space under control and entered his office to research this area.

I punched in facts about Wyoming and decided that we'd have to make a trip further west before we left to see Yellowstone, the geysers and Grand Tetons. I spent hours crafting a travel itinerary. At lunchtime, I got up and observed unique landscapes from each window. The sky was clear, and the sun radiated warmth through the windows. I threw on a coat and stepped outside to feel it on my face. As I leaned over the railing, taking deep breaths of fresh air, I saw movement out of my peripheral vision. Oh, hell no.

A bear sniffed around the tree where the deer hung last night. I stepped back toward the door and it saw me move. It lifted its gigantic head and flared its nostrils. I froze. It was only a couple of steps back inside, but I stood paralyzed. My insides quivered, and I fought to keep all my intestinal sphincters operating. The bear grunted as it circled the tree, still glancing my way, until it stopped, facing me.

I told myself to get inside but was still incapable of movement. He swung his head from side to side and charged toward me. Electricity shot through me as I screamed an ungodly noise and tried to jump through the closed door. In the nick of time, I opened it, turned to lock it and slammed it in the bear's face. He was so big he stressed the porch boards. And the noise he made breathing was terrifying. I crawled on the floor to get my guns. All of them. Death awaited him if he dared to enter through a window.

I wondered what bears do after they smell blood? I called Eddie and asked what I should do?

Wayne said in the background, "Shoot it now, or it will keep coming back. It will hang around until it eats."

Eddie said, "Leave the phone on speaker. You can do it. We're an hour away, so you have to take care of it."

Wayne was talking in the background about what gun to use.

I yelled, "I'm going to use them all!" I didn't see him when I looked out on the porch. "Did he leave?"

"Grab meat from the fridge and toss it out the door," Wayne said. "He'll come running."

I tossed the unfrozen deer chunk over the railing. And waited. I opened a front window and stuck my barrel out before he came back. He grunted while lumbering towards the meat, swinging his massive head, bouncing side to side.

I shot as soon as he got in front of me. The shotgun blew the railing apart into a hundred pieces. I kept shooting until the bear was down and the railing was history. Trembling, I rose to grab the phone and inform them of the bear's demise.

Eddie laughed and asked, "How many were there, Rae? Did you keep missing it?"

I didn't think it was funny.

I said, "I fucking hate bears." And hung up.

In slightly more than an hour, they arrived. I watched them out the window as they looked at the dead bear and porch. Wayne walked over to the shed and pulled a sled back behind him. They moved the bear onto it and pulled it inside the shed. He lit a pot in front of the shed that gave off blue smoke before they came inside.

"Look, I'm sorry about the porch. Obviously, it was necessary."

Wayne held his laugh in. "Fucking bears."

Eddie said, "Did you count your shots? I mean, I never saw a Swiss cheese bear before."

I threw a pillow at him and told him, "Shut up. I could've died!"

He gave me a side hug and told me I did well, but if I listened to him about staying inside, this wouldn't have happened. I was still traumatized and rethinking my plan to explore more of Wyoming, certain I'll never step foot outside without a weapon ever again.

Wayne said he'd make dinner tonight as Eddie told me about their meetings today. Wayne walked back and forth in the kitchen, opening drawers and scratching his head. Eddie looked at me, like really?

"Um, Wayne, I promise I'll put them all back before we leave. It's a thing I do. Sorry." He scratched his head again and went on with dinner preparations.

I asked Eddie if he had any fresh information regarding the events in Binghamton.

"They keep uncovering more corruption. Not all related to the radical group, some of it just politics. Mayor Devine dug in deep and probably made a few new enemies."

She made a lasting impression on me for the little time I knew her. "I bet she'll get it all figured out. Seems like she'll regroup and come out fighting. Any estimate on when we'll finish there?"

He shook his head no.

Wayne called us into the kitchen area and regaled us with his hunting stories and close calls with the wildlife here while we ate. With full bellies, we waddled off to bed.

DAY TWENTY-FIVE

Wayne suggested using the ATVs to explore more of the area in the morning. I was enjoying my coffee with creamer this morning, looking out the front windows. I glanced at Eddie for confirmation.

He replied, "We haven't made plans with anyone else, so we're available. And for Rae's benefit, the ATVs are faster than all the wildlife."

I gave him a dirty look. "Don't even start with me. I've never shot an animal, let alone one that big. And obviously, my fear isn't unfounded since it tried to kill me."

He sighed. "You're so dramatic."

Wayne laughed and said we acted like siblings.

With a wink, I quipped, "Yes, the brothers I never desired."

I carried as many weapons and as much ammo as I could before hopping on Wayne's ATV. Despite driving through hills, creeks, tall grass, and dirt fields, we saw no creatures. At the hill's peak, we stopped to appreciate the scenery and hydrate. As we stood talking, Eddie slowly took his rifle out of the sling. Wayne and I turned to see what had caught his attention, but found nothing.

I whispered, "What is it?"

He handed me his gun and said, "A little family." I found the mountain lion with her three cubs playing near a bunch of trees and rocks.

"Ah, look how cute they are. So little."

Wayne advised we get out of there and leave her alone.

We took a different path home, using up all the morning hours. Once inside, Wayne rubbed some ointment on his hands and offered it to us.

"Takes care of arthritis pain better than anything you can get in the store."

Without hesitation, I applied it to my hands where the monsters had hammered nails through them. He grabbed my hand to inspect it, turning it over, and back again, feeling the scars under my tattoos. He waited for me to tell him.

"The head terrorist drove two nails into my hand. While he raped me."

He blinked and shuddered but didn't comment. He shook his head as he walked over to the sink and pulled a mason jar out from under it and handed it to me.

"Let me know when you need more."

Eddie walked out of the room when his phone rang. It was a jovial conversation, and I overheard him say bear a couple of times. He walked back in and handed me the phone.

I hesitantly took it and said, "Hello."

Joe said, "Hey, bear killer. Are you ok?"

I walked out of the room to tell him about my harrowing experience. He told me they were working overtime to wrap it up in Binghamton, but it was like playing whack-a-mole.

"We keep finding other groups that are linked to the original group, even if they weren't aware. It all comes back to money, like everything else, but we'll get it taken care of soon. I promise."

It couldn't be soon enough for me. "Finish up so you can join me out here. Don't worry about me, I can even kill a bear. I miss you."

Joe hung up after he said, "Love you, Rae."

I rejoined them in the living room and handed Eddie his phone back. He and Wayne discussed our safety-enhancing inventions. Wayne asked detailed questions about them and how they worked. He said his formal education was in chemistry but showed his versatility through the greenhouse he built.

Pointing to my head, I stated, "I still have plenty of ideas. Perhaps you could help bring them to life?" The idea of veterans producing these items occurred to me. Safety tools for home use and professional use. Wayne is the ideal candidate to manage the place.

Eddie looked at his phone and read aloud the profiles of a five more vets in the area. Because of financial issues, three choices were eliminated. Wayne asked why?

"Because we don't need any sell outs in this unit. If someone volunteers to fix your money issues by killing one of us, or getting to our clients, that's too risky."

Wayne responded, "Yeah, it wouldn't be a stretch to kill someone for money. A lot of retired guys are mercenaries. It's not a big leap."

Eddie said, "It's a different breed that does that. Working for whoever pays them the most, killing for someone else's cause. Those deeply involved are the ones who have witnessed and committed such atrocities that they believe the number of lives they take no longer holds any significance. There's no redemption for them."

He acted like he understood, but I didn't. Serving as a soldier, sacrificing your life for your country should differ completely from killing for financial gain, shouldn't it?

An alarm beeped, prompting Wayne to get up and glance out the window. He touched the holster on hip and shook his head.

"You guys stay out of sight."

He grabbed his jacket and met the owner of the jacked-up pickup outside.

Eddie motioned for me to follow. "Come on, let's check him out."

In silence, we departed via the back door and positioned ourselves by the house to eavesdrop. The guy with a southern accent talked much louder than Wayne and got louder as the conversation continued. It ended with him slamming the truck door and throwing rocks as he sped back down the driveway. We crept out front and saw Wayne standing there, running both hands through his very short hair.

Turning around, he informed us, "That crazy bastard caught wind of some work and wants to be a part of it. He has the potential to become a problem."

I speculated, "So could whoever told him?"

Wayne stomped his foot and said, "Fuck, fuck, fuck."

Eddie sent the guy's full name and info to Mickey to check out and keep track of. Wayne made calls to Ritt and Andy to ask who they've talked to about us. They swore they didn't tell anyone.

Wayne paced in front of the kitchen island, running his hands over the bar stools as he walked. "Got to be at the diner. I bet it was a waitress with big ears that knows him." He rubbed his nose and came up with her name to run a background on.

Wayne strode purposefully to a cabinet, grabbed a bottle of bourbon, and poured three glasses. With his full glass, he slowly lowered himself to his recliner and had a few gulps like it was water. The sip I took made my nose burn and eyes water.

He saw me shudder and said, "You get used to it."

Eddie was holding his glass in one hand, the phone in the other. His finger was flicking the screen to read it as fast as possible.

"What is it?"

He glanced at me and said, "Nothing good."

Wayne gulped the rest of his drink and filled his glass up again.

"How about I heat the leftovers?" I didn't wait for an answer and busied myself in the kitchen. I couldn't help but think all this was my fault. I shouldn't have agreed to go back to New York. That's what started this again. Like it woke up the hornets' nest. What was the price of my life? How is it possible for so many individuals to be aware of my existence and desire my demise? I filled up my glass again and sipped it until the warmth of it soothed me.

I brought plates into the living room. Wayne held his plate on his chest and shoveled it in his mouth. Once he finished, he took our three plates to the kitchen and washed them. After asking if we wanted more bourbon, he promptly put the bottle away.

"I have a two-glass limit."

Eddie said, "Good to know."

He waited for Wayne to sit down again to read the report Mickey sent. "They both have some shitty credit scores. Both rent, have multiple previous addresses, and have some known felon contacts."

Wayne asked, "You got all that information that quick?"

I said, "Mickey is the best at finding stuff, however he does it."

Wayne leaned forward. "Their potential to bring trouble is now probable. I don't think he's too stable. Actually, I think he's pretty fucked up. She's worked at the diner for years, never really liked her. I've always thought she did favors for the owner, if you get my drift." He sat back and asked, "What's the plan? Do we neutralize the presumed threat or wait it out?"

Eddie set down his drink and phone. "I think we should gather more information about them. Do you think Ritt and Andy will do some recon for us? See if they're working together? At present, it seems this is solely about profit and has no ties to Rae's history."

I was relieved to hear that.

Wayne stood up and showed us the way to the safe room. He showed us all the secrets the room held, the computer password, hidden guns, shields, a drawer of MREs, and an escape hatch to the roof and one under the house. It was a smaller version of the greenhouse and just as cool.

He shut the light off and said, "Best to be prepared for the worst. I'll see you in the morning."

Eddie and I sat up a little longer. He pulled up a picture of the waitress and joked, "You think you can take her?" I grabbed his phone to check her out.

"Well, it appears she's had a hard life and doesn't have any muscles in her long, skinny arms. You never know about desperate people, though. She could be a rough one."

He snickered. "Bet you'd outrun her and leave her to a bear, wouldn't you?"

With confidence, I said, "That's a big 10-4."

"Goodnight, brother Eddie."

DAY TWENTY-SIX

I stayed cuddled under the blankets until I had to get up to pee. The house was quiet when I drifted into the kitchen for coffee. I looked out the front window and saw that Wayne's truck was gone and yelled for Eddie. He didn't answer, so I yelled again as I walked through the house. Then I heard him pound down on the ceiling. He's probably examining the roof hatch. He stuck his head down the opening and yelled for me to come up.

"Check this shit out."

He happily showed me the fully stocked pigeon hole that was behind the dormer that overlooked the front of the house.

"He was really thoughtful when he revamped this house. Every room needs a sign that says, in case of emergency."

All of it amazed me. "Wonder why he planned all of this? What was he expecting to happen?"

Eddie said, "That's the point. He's ready for anything. Probably all the things he wished he had when he was deployed. I think he'll be valuable to FETCH. Especially to our clients that need to beef up their security and design at home."

"Let's go check out the ground hatch."

I followed Eddie down the stairs and into the crawl space under the house. We laid on our bellies and looked around with flashlights. Eddie shone his beam on all the pillars of the house.

"Notice the size difference between those two compared to the rest. I bet he's got something inside them. Let's check."

We army-crawled over to inspect them. My elbow landed on something hard. After some digging, I found a Phillips head screwdriver. He grabbed it and unscrewed the wood around the big pillar.

"No way. Look down here. It's a tunnel." He flashed his light down the wooden stairs and said, "Stay here. I'll be right back." His light beam disappeared and came back a minute later. "It goes to the shed, comes up in the corner."

As we army crawled back, he mentioned, "Good thing it's too cold for those rattlesnakes to be awake under here."

I reached the ladder before him to escape.

"Gear up, we're going for a walk. I want to explore the area behind the house. Put your vest on over your coat."

I scoffed. "You don't have to tell me twice. I'll be carrying my bear spray."

We stopped to appreciate the beauty that surrounded us. "It's so perfect it looks fake."

He pointed toward Yellowstone and said, "You'll be stunned when we go through the park. Absolute raw beauty."

I smiled and expressed my need for a real camera. It's no surprise that this scenery is popular on calendars.

Eddie tied a rope around my waist and gestured towards a rock formation that looked impossible for me to climb.

"We should get a higher view."

I looked again. "Maybe you should look from up there. I'll wait here." I started to untie the rope, but he yanked me forward before I could.

"Just follow in my footsteps. You'll be fine."

I growled, "Well, you need to make smaller steps, remember my legs aren't as long as yours."

He found a crevice that was rough enough to act as steps and handholds.

"There's a plateau up about ten feet to rest."

We sat to survey all that was around us. The house looked tiny from this vantage point. Eddie raised his hand to signal silence, then turned his head to locate the source of the falling rocks. I was afraid to look.

I whispered, "What is it?" He pushed my hand down that was ready with bear spray.

"Big horn sheep. They're typically not aggressive. Stay still and watch how they navigate the rocks."

After briefly locking eyes on us, they quickly bounded away.

He stood up and took pictures with his phone and sent them to Mickey. "They'll be excited to come out and hunt."

The wildlife made me nervous. Everything was gigantic. I'd be a shoot first and ask questions later on all of them.

Eddie debated going higher, but I intervened with a firm "No!" We descended the plateau, maneuvering through boulders and grass until we reached the edge of Wayne's property.

Eddie proposed, "Here's an idea. Next year, for Christmas, you purchase a place out here. Not complaining about the truck, but we'd all enjoy a lodge here. Just saying."

He tapped my shoulder and winked, and we kept walking. I would probably do exactly what he suggested. Despite his lighthearted comment, I was certain everyone would appreciate having a place in this area. Last year I bought them all pickups for Christmas. My money was useless if I couldn't spoil my only family.

We met Wayne in the driveway as he pulled up. He opened the tailgate and asked us to lend a hand.

"I visited every store in town, conversed with everyone I knew, and even a few I didn't. The skanky waitress at the diner was unusually friendly when she served me. Hell, she even volunteered to service me." He shuddered at the thought. "Come on, let's get inside and I'll tell you all about it."

We each grabbed a few bags and followed him to the kitchen.

Eddie and I unpacked the bags while he put them away. He was clearly pleased with himself by the way he was humming.

"So, tell us already, you big stud."

He shuddered again and offered us a beer. We stood at the kitchen island as he told us exactly who and where he talked to people.

"They were particularly chatty today. Seems the waitress will do almost anything because of her financial struggles. Chris has advertised his openness to do anything to earn money. Although he mostly offers legitimate services, he's not opposed to engaging in illicit activities. Most town folk get a bad vibe from him and hope he just moves on." He drank half his beer in a couple gulps. "I think he's got some bad habits that he came by from his experiences. Doesn't excuse him, but explains it."

Eddie inquired, "If we found him a job elsewhere, would that solve the issue?"

I asked about the girl. "Won't she keep looking for ways to make money? She seems like she'd stoop lower than him."

Eddie took his phone and texted Mickey to look for jobs for them out of town.

Wayne pondered, "Is it workable for them to team up with a rodeo?"

Eddie told Wayne what we did today and apologized if we overstepped, but safety was his chief concern here.

"I've got to tell you, Wayne, you planned this house out so well. I'm certain our clients would benefit from your designs. Once we get the team out here locked down and trained for our backup, we'll get you started on designing safe rooms for our clients."

Wayne raised his bottle to Eddie and clinked it.

"You didn't design this house, but you've done a lot of renovations. Did you have trouble out here?"

I couldn't imagine that way out in the middle of nowhere he would.

Wayne pointed to the living room. We followed him as he put his feet up in his recliner.

"I expanded on the safety features inside, obviously. Other ideas came to me while I was overseas. They had tunnel systems that worked pretty well for sneaking around and I tried to improve upon that idea. I'm not one of the crazy preppers, but you can never predict what will happen on our soil. If something occurs, I want to be alive to hold the perpetrators accountable. I'll wait in the greenhouse until it's safe to come out fighting."

This guy really was brilliant.

"I've met enough misguided Americans to realize anything can happen. Every country has its share of crazies." I touched the bruise on my face and said, "This happened on base. One of our soldiers granted access to the person responsible for attacking me. He thought he knew who I was and what I supposedly represent. Fools."

Wayne shook his head and asked, "Did he end up worse than you, like you said when we met?"

Eddie volunteered, "She cut his dick off while she stabbed him to death."

Wayne squeezed his legs shut and looked at me for confirmation.

I shrugged and said, "He was trying to rape me before he killed me. So. Yeah." I realized how callous I was when I blurted that out. "I'm certainly not proud of that. But these zealots keep trying to kill me."

Eddie stood up and said, "You should be proud. When it's a kill or be killed situation, you don't hesitate or you die. You weren't like this before you were attacked, so whatever happens to that group gets what they deserve."

Wayne put his recliner down and rubbed his leg before going to the kitchen. Noticing our curious glances, he disclosed, "Took a shot in the leg. When I'm up on it a lot, it swells, so I put it up whenever I can." He opened the fridge and said, "How about we throw some meat on the grill?" He sorted out three big potatoes to go with it.

We made a fire in the firepit while Wayne cooked dinner in the dark. I finally convinced myself to stop worrying about bears and enjoy the perfectly clear, starlit night. I crouched in the chair to save myself from craning my neck to see the sky. My back got so chilly I had to stand with it to the fire. My mouth dropped in awe of the mountains when I looked behind the house. The sky over them was an odd shade of green that seemed to move.

Wayne stood beside me, tongues in hand, saying, "That's glory."

I understood what he meant, but I was curious how the sky could be that color.

"It's stunning."

We ate outside and stayed by the fire, watching the sky until bedtime.

DAY TWENTY-SEVEN

I woke up to Eddie nudging me, sitting on my bed, holding the TV remote in his hand. "You've got to see this." He nudged me again. "Sit up." He grabbed the extra pillows and propped back on the headboard. I pulled the covers with me as I propped up.

It was national news from Binghamton, NY. Fiery scenes, people in handcuffs, images of downtown and a few rural settings, tables of weapons on display and finally what must have been the closing words of Mayor Michelle Devine. "It was a concerted effort of many agencies to eradicate or imprison these terrorists and criminals. We promise to diligently serve the people and take action against terrorist groups. Thank you. God Bless."

"Does this mean it's over?" He made his eyebrows go high and said, "Duh." He clicked the TV off and left my room. I joyfully rose, showered, and joined them in the kitchen. I left my wig on the counter and spiked up my hair.

Wayne did a double take, nodded and smiled. I thought out loud, "I hope it's not bad karma that I'm glad those monsters are either dead or in jail? But I really hope they got them all. And it sounds like they got corrupt government people too. Guess we all face the consequences, eventually."

Eddie said, "Once you cross the line in any part of your life, you understand that. You know you're going to pay the price one day. Unlike most people, the evil ones are unconcerned about the collateral damage they cause."

Wayne softly said, "They sure don't care over there. I've seen them hold babies up in front of themselves as shields. You know, for their cause." Over his coffee cup he added, "Good thing when you shoot their legs out from under them, they drop the child so you can get a better shot." Damn. They both agreed they were good with the karma they'll get.

I finished my cup and said, "Good vs Evil, right? Just stay on the right side."

Eddie slid his phone over to me. "Be there soon, helping with loose ends." I did a happy dance all over the house.

Wayne said another guy they were considering for the team could meet us today.

Eddie asked if I was ok staying here by myself, again. "Please stay inside and don't go looking for trouble. Consider sitting in the safe room." Wayne assured him I'd be fine in there, and they left for town.

I sat down with another cup of coffee at Waynes' computer to search real estate for sale, knowing the guys would enjoy a retreat here. Several listings in the vicinity featured 50 acres of land. Should I buy one and surprise them or wait for them to decide which one to get? I printed a map to follow even though the GPS in the truck worked; I wondered how far it would get a signal.

I looked for the keys to our truck as I thought about it. Eddie left them on the kitchen bar. Could I get back before they did? Was it considered looking for trouble? I armed myself with all my guns and grabbed my rifle for the truck. I wrote three addresses and left a note on the computer as a precaution. In case they got back before me. Or, well, just in case. I felt confident defending myself and wanted to find the perfect retreat to gift the guys.

Before opening the door, I checked outside to avoid surprising a smokey. I only saw the pickup coming up the driveway after I opened the door. I slammed the door shut and ran back to the computer room. I doubt the driver saw me, but I wasn't sure. The motion activated camera blinked and beeped. That guy named Chris got out of his truck. Another figure sat in the passenger seat. I called Eddie, left a message, and texted him, and sent Mickey a text too, then I put my phone on silent.

I watched Chis look inside our truck and try to open the doors. The passenger got out and towered over Chris, and I hated my luck. I took pictures of the screen and sent it to Eddie and Mickey. Eddie texted back. GET IN SAFE ROOM. Another alarm sounded. It was for the back door. I checked the screen again and saw both guys. How did a third one bypass the monitor? I should be better at this.

My top priority was reaching the safe room. Holding my gun, I cautiously moved down the hall until a powerful shot shattered the door, then I sprinted the rest of the way. I gently closed the door to avoid giving away my location. Should I go up or down? There was total silence in this room. They must have turned the power off. I was certain Wayne had backup power here, but where exactly? Was there a switch? When I was halfway down the chute, the power chirped on. I didn't have time to check the monitors; I had to get out.

As I army crawled under the house, booms exploded all over the house. Were they nuts? Why were they doing this to Wayne's house? The house shook above me, and I wondered if it was going to cave in on top of me. I reached the pillar that led to the tunnel and loosened the screws, using a screwdriver and my fingers. I leaned the panel back against the pillar, but I didn't have time to screw it shut. I slid down the ladder and started running as soon as I hit the floor until I reached the shed.

Before exiting the tunnel, I listened from the top of the stairs. The noise from the house continued with reverberating booms and bangs. I'll be sure to thank Wayne for being prepared if I escape. I had to leave the shed and move away from the house. I opened the window opposite of the house away and crawled out. I peeked around both sides of the shed, hopefully hidden by it, and bolted away from the house.

When I reached a thick gathering of trees and rocks, I stopped and turned to look behind me. I'd end up at the road if I kept going. If I turned left, I'd have to cross the driveway. Since turning back wasn't an option, I ventured further up into the hills, where the threats surpassed armed men.

The booming sounds gradually diminished. I glanced behind me every so often, but since the house was out of view, I knew they weren't able to see me. I stuck close to bigger rock formations and zig-zagged my way up the mountain. After five minutes, my legs were throbbing, and I had to sit. I pulled out my phone and correctly guessed there would be no signal.

I had a clear view of the house over the trees and checked behind me towards my destination. It's likely a five or ten-minute climb, considering there's no running involved anymore.

It had been less than a half hour since this started, meaning Eddie and Wayne would be at least another half hour until they got back. What a mess they'd return to. Poor Wayne would now have first-hand knowledge of the shit-show surrounding me.

Perched on a plateau, I saw the house and the telltale sign of someone leaving the driveway. The dirt rising followed the truck as it left. I sat down and succumbed to guilt. This is the shit that happens to people that care and support my cause. I should come with a disclaimer notice.

The signal bars on my phone were absent, and I'm still undecided about which direction to take. Back to the house? Did they all leave? Go toward the road? Along the ridgeline behind the house? Certainly not over the mountain. The summit remained a few hundred feet away.

The hand holding my phone told me how I really felt. It was shaking. It's hard to say where I'd be without Wayne's room. Hostage? Dead? Definitely wounded. These guys were simply seeking money. I don't understand how a vet could attack another vet, though. Seems like a code they shouldn't break. How they destroyed the house seems unhinged. They were very dangerous and I hope they didn't meet Wayne and Eddie on the road. Once Wayne sees his house, they better keep driving.

I plodded across the hillside, constantly scanning for man and beast. Eventually, I found the spot where Eddie and I climbed the other day. I questioned whether I could descend instead of ascend.

I sat down, sheltered by a group of trees to survey the house, shed and greenhouse. I wish I had binoculars as I was still several football fields away from the house and very elevated. The sun was bright and streaky, and also dense and cold. How was it possible for it to feel so different? The rocks absorbed it; the trees filtered it and it moved in the tall oat colored grass.

The house was moving as I watched it. The roof was swaying and crumbling in on itself. Eddie and Wayne drove up just in time to witness it. They got out of the truck as the house finally gave up and collapsed. They were so focused on the house they didn't notice the two guys running toward them from the greenhouse. The dense dust blocked my view, but they were gone once it cleared. The truck and the men.

I was sure I saw their truck leave, the sneaky bastards. Now they had Wayne's truck and theirs. Still no phone signal from where I sat. Sizing up the gap I was about to crawl down, I chose to avoid breaking a leg via that route and ran down the hillside instead.

I sprinted at maximum speed with all the extra gear on. I needed a phone signal to call in reinforcements to get Eddie and Wayne back. The sun glaring into my teary eyes wasn't helping me avoid all the animal poop I kept stepping and sliding in. Falling in a pile of it would be gross.

Positioned behind the greenhouse, I checked my phone again. Why isn't there a signal? It seems the house Wi-Fi was not working and cell towers were few and far between. I had the keys to our truck and thought I'd make a run for it until I saw the flat tires. Dammit. Then I remembered the ATVs. I rushed to the shed, ensured the one I took had gas, and sped down the driveway towards town. With little traffic, I stayed on the road to maintain a higher speed. Would the gas last the entire hour-long trip to town? I had the throttle at max speed and acknowledged without a helmet my brain would be mush if I crashed.

A game warden pickup passed me, going the other way. Shit, a cop. Eddie told me they have a lot of power out here and I resembled Rambo going to town. Sure enough, he spun around and hit his lights and advanced on me quickly. I had a rifle hanging off my back and was speeding on an ATV. I stopped and shed the rifle, waiting for him to exit his truck. With a megaphone, he commanded me to face away and raise my arms. Stepping out of his vehicle, he repeated himself. He told me to walk backwards with my feet wide and asked if I had more weapons. What do I do? See if he finds them or tell the truth and possibly go to jail? He screamed the question again, but before I answered him, he tased me in the leg. I fell face first onto the road and grabbed my hamstring, that was in spasm. Christ, that hurt.

He approached slowly, telling me not to move. When he stood over me, he said, "Hello, Rachel. Nice to see you again."

I tried to reach for my ankle holster, but he kicked my hands away. I grabbed his boot, twisted it, and lifted his foot in the air, knocking him off balance. He turned his body and kicked full force into my stomach. He used his foot to roll me over as I gasped for air, then fell on me with his knee on my back. He tightened a handcuff on my wrist as I fought to get my other hand underneath me.

A car slowed down and stopped to ask the officer if he needed help. I screamed. "He's not a cop. Call 911, call FETCH, call."

Without hesitation, he shot the man inside his vehicle, warning, "Try that again, and more innocent people will die because of you." I was stunned long enough for him to pull my arm and get the other cuff on me, then he hauled me to my feet. I kicked him and kicked him, but dear old Uncle Roger kept pushing me toward his truck. He shoved me up against the door and put a cloth over my nose.

"Sweet Dreams."

DAY TWENTY-EIGHT

Was it morning or night? It was dark, wherever I was, so I couldn't tell. And where was he? Sitting, watching me in the dark? Fuck-wad. I laid still another a few minutes until I fully woke up. No handcuffs. I think that's a bad sign; it means he knows I can't escape. I held my hand in front of my face and didn't see it. I stretched to confirm that I wasn't buried alive, and that there was ample space around me. Now what? Wait for him to come back? He could be sitting two feet away, and I wouldn't know. I rolled off my back, got to my knees, and stood up. I was wearing a harness with a long rope attached. The nylon harness was tight under my legs and around my torso. I reeled in the rope attached to me until I held the end in my hand. I threw it all away from me and reeled it in again, measuring it with my arm span to figure it was about sixty feet.

I sat back down and bit my knuckles to keep from screaming out. Am I that far underground? Did he imprison me in an inescapable cave? It was so dark I couldn't even blink any light in. If I didn't get up and move, I'd scream.

I scuffed a hole in the dirt to determine my starting point, if I made it back to here. With arms outstretched, I counted my steps to make a square, then kept going further each time, five steps in all directions, then six, seven, eight, until I hit a wall. I ran my hand along the dirty, rocky rough texture. I was in a hole. A tunnel? An old mine? I searched the darkness for a smidgeon of light, but found only blackness. I used my elbow to make an indent in the wall and dragged my hand on the wall until I got back to my starting point. I took 31 long steps around the perimeter. So how big was this hole? Who needs math? My conclusion is that it's pretty big. I walked it again, reaching high and low, searching for anything that will help. It would be wonderful to stumble upon a ladder or light. A dream, of course.

Plan it, work it, time it. That slogan works when you know what you're dealing with and you're not scared to death. I felt petrified.

I kept counting, which kept my anxiety in check and kept walking, running my hands on the wall. Large patches of stone co-mingled with hardened dirt as I ran my fingers along the surface of my tomb. Hours ticked by until the smallest glimmer of light shone above me. Way above me. There was a wooden trellis looking structure on the walls, nearly twenty feet above me that stretched up to top. I needed more light to devise my plan for reaching up there. I checked myself for anything useful. All my weapons were gone, but holy shit, he left my belt on me? I pulled at my buckle for the knife inside, but that was gone. I could use the buckle anyway. I wondered if I could catch the harness on the wood and pull myself up? I threw it in the air towards the wood's edges, but the tightness against the walls prevented the harness from catching onto anything. I put the harness back on after rewinding it. I didn't want to lose track of it and panic.

I pulled my belt through my loops, then wound it around my fist to get a good solid hold on the buckle. I'll scrape the edge of the buckle to carve foot and handholds in the wall. As the sun shone brighter, my plan took shape. I dug the walls deep so I could fit my foot in without cutting out. Once

I hit my carving limit on the ground, I had to simultaneously climb and scrape. My hands cramped and my hamstring was still sore from the taser. I fell off the wall when I was about two feet off the ground. I paused to pity myself, then got back up. With the growing light, I continued onwards despite the slow pace. When I tried to hurry, my hand cramped faster, making me return to slow and methodical movements. Failing to reach the top before dark would be disastrous.

More light revealed beams across the opening. I'd gnaw through them if I had to. If I get that far. My dug-out crevices were closer together the higher I got. My whole body was vibrating with muscle cramps, nerves and flat-out fear. I'd slap myself if I had a free hand. Get your shit together, Rachel. Do you want to die? No! Keep moving, keep digging.

Finally, I reached the lowest rung on the trellis. Despite the pain in my pink and raw fingertips, I found a fingerhold and pulled myself up higher. My feet were on the bottom rung as I plastered myself to the wall and carefully grabbed the rope from around my shoulder and neck. I slid the rope between the wall and wood and tied it off tight. I completely relaxed and let the harness take my full weight as I hung on the side of the mining hole.

Aware of the limited time before the sun dimmed, I gazed at its peak brightness. Its rays came through the beams at the top in a checkerboard pattern. With my feet supporting me again, I untied myself, rolled the rope around my head and shoulder. I left a small piece for me to use when I needed a break or for extra safety when I was making a leap because they made these damn beams for giants. I shimmied sideways on the trellis to catch the vertical beams when the horizontal ones were too far for me to reach. Whoever built this didn't use a level or measuring tape because I had to keep moving around the sides of the hole instead of a straight climb. The sides of it were all rock now, making it impossible to dig any more spots in between to hold.

My arms were aching from the overhead pulling, my legs were shaking and my stomach was nauseas from holding my core tight to the wall. I still had twenty or thirty feet to go, and I wondered if it was physically possible for me to keep climbing. I tied off to rest again. And pray.

Having reconciled with God, I didn't stop climbing until I reached the top. The beams covering the hole lay in a pattern but weren't nailed. With every ounce of strength I had left, I tied off and struggled to push the heavy beams aside, creating enough space for me to crawl out.

The brown grass was tall all around me, letting me hide, rest and gather up the rope again. I sat up to survey my surroundings, which looked untouched, and I wondered if he dropped me from a helicopter. Standing, I still didn't see any trails leading to my site. The roads must have disappeared since the past drilling. The vast wilderness offered no direction, no guiding beacon in sight. I had to choose a path with hiding spots in case he returned, which I assumed he would. Scouring the ground near the mine's top, I sought a potential weapon. I found one rusty nail that I'd probably get tetanus from, so I left it there. I tried to remember the landscape I saw the other day while I vacation planned. I vaguely remember reading about mining for minerals and seeing the spots on maps where they were and used to be. It seems there were a few north of Wayne's house that were closed.

As the sun set in the west, I glanced at the mountains on my right to gauge my location before heading downhill towards the south. Straining my eyes, I searched for any movement - man or beast - with each step. I jogged when the land was flat. I maneuvered through random rock formations, opting to go over rather than around. Wyoming's terrain was unusually unique. My thoughts were on Eddie being alive and the location of FETCH.

Luckily for me, the moon was going to be full tonight to help light my way. My thoughts ran wild about why Roger would leave me there alive? So, he had the option to tell me he's killed my entire team and taunt me as I slowly die in a hole? The hatred for him lit a fire under my feet and I double-timed it as Eddie would say, and jogged for miles. I focused on my breathing, my love for Joe, and the chance to kill Roger.

I was high atop another outcropping when I spied the glittering lights of a small city. Feeling relieved about heading in the right direction, I shifted my focus to plan my actions upon arrival. Who could I trust? They took Wayne and Eddie. Were Ritt and Andy safe? Did they act alone, or was Uncle Roger involved? The howling wolves scared the crap and the fatigue out of me. I ran until I reached the city limits.

Behind the first commercial building at the town's edge, I stopped to remove my harness and rope. It was an auto repair place that sold tires, judging by the stacks of them that sat in front of the building. The adrenaline or fear that drove me this far was dissipating. I wedged myself in between two towers of tires in front of the building so I could see traffic while I rested and if I stood, the main drag of town was visible. Luckily, there was some warmth stuck between the rubber and cement of the building. My underclothes were cold with sweat, but my hands and face were cold. I took my jacket off to dry out a bit but covered my head with it to keep my body heat in. I kept flicking my clothes to air them until I was too tired to move.

DAY TWENTY-NINE

Are you shitting me? Looking at my feet in the cocoon, I realized it was already daylight. At least the beginning of it. The element of surprise and nighttime cover is gone. I blew that. How incompetent could I be? What if I was too late to help Eddie?

The sound of the big garage door opening presented my only option. Get inside to use the phone without him seeing me, and, or hope that he's a good guy and helps me. I walked behind the wall of tires to get a look inside. Why didn't the employee resemble a dweeb rather than a motorcycle gang leader? I fluffed my hair up and walked into the garage.

"Good morning. I hope your day is better than mine." He jerked his head up, scowled, then relaxed his face.

"What can I do for you?" I didn't get the warm fuzzies from him, but I didn't want to run either.

"It seems I've got some car troubles and need to call a friend for help. Can I use your phone?" He looked around his garage like I should ask him to fix my car.

He stepped forward. "Maybe you don't need to call anybody." I stepped back, about to run when he said, "Maybe I can help you and save your friend a trip."

I exhaled and smiled. "No, don't want to inconvenience you. I just need to call them. So, can I use your phone?" There was no point in trying to flirt with him since I looked like a filthy, abandoned mutt. He reached into his pocket and pulled out his phone and handed it to me. I snatched it and walked backwards to the front of the garage.

I called Joe, left a message, followed by Mickey, then JD. I had to wrack my brain to remember numbers instead of automatically dialing their numbers. JD answered, and I spilled all the details. He mentioned the team hadn't taken off, so he couldn't provide an ETA yet. No word on Eddie. He intended to contact Ritt and Andy, requesting their assistance in picking me up. His parting words were, "Rachel, don't engage with Roger by yourself."

The big guy was looking at me in the reflection of the huge glass window, but I pretended to keep talking and walked in circles. I meandered towards a car was on a lift and casually kicked some tools around on the floor. I glanced at him every so often and watched him mill around. I picked up a four-way lug wrench and twirled it like a baton. I made eye contact with him and smiled as I walked behind the car on the lift to delete the calls I made so he wasn't able to check the numbers.

Ritt's pickup nearly slid inside the open garage door. He opened his door but stood behind it. He yelled hello to the big guy and asked where his visitor was. I handed the guy's phone back and thanked him before I hopped in the passenger side of Ritt's truck. We left as fast as he pulled in.

"Have you heard from Wayne or Eddie? What's happening?"

He shook his head. "Those assholes just called me, said to get into Wayne's account and bring them all the money. We're going to the bank now."

I was relieved to know they didn't know my real identity and were only concerned with money. It wasn't my fault. I picked his phone off the console and called JD to give him an update. I put him on speaker for Ritt to give him more details. JD emphasized to Ritt that this was a high alert situation because of Uncle Roger. The major threat wasn't with Wayne and Eddie. Once he discovered I was gone, he'd be more hellbent to find me and the team. Maybe he'd make a mistake.

Ritt reached into the backseat for a furry hat with ear flaps for me to put on while he stormed inside the bank. He lay a shotgun in my lap and handed me a pistol before he got out. "Stay low and stay ready."

I wanted to say this isn't my first rodeo, instead I shook my head affirmatively. After twelve minutes, Ritt walked out of the bank with a duffle bag. Now, we had to wait for a phone call with the exchange location. After leaving the bank, we drove to the end of town and pulled over to wait. I kept the furry hat on to combat the chill I still had from yesterday.

An hour later, we were still waiting. Ritt rubbed his temples and said, "Wayne's a stand-up guy, and the smartest guy I know. Is it likely that they escaped from wherever they were being held?"

I agreed. "That's definitely a possibility. I wouldn't put it past Eddie to get away either. Maybe that's why they haven't called."

Another fifteen minutes before the phone rang. It was Wayne. "Go put my damn money back in the bank. We'll meet you there."

I asked, "Where's Eddie?" "He's right here. See you soon."

Ritt seemed relieved but questioned, "That seemed legitimate, didn't it?" He put the truck in drive and returned to the bank.

I offered, "We'll have the answer soon."

Wayne and Eddie stood outside the bank and it didn't occur to me they weren't aware of Uncle Roger until just now. I was running to Eddie before the truck stopped to tell him. He and I got back in Ritt's pickup to wait for Wayne to redeposit his fortune. I recounted Uncle Roger's actions, my escape, and not having an ETA for the team. "Why wouldn't he kill me unless he was planning on torturing me with your deaths before I died?" Before he could respond, they hopped back into the truck.

Ritt started it and asked, "Where to?"

Eddie said, "Get some gas. We're going on a road trip."

Ritt looked at me in the rear-view mirror. "I filled him in on your uncle while we were inside."

Wayne gave directions to another small piece of property he had. "It's very rudimentary. And it's not held in my name, should anyone be looking for my holdings. It's been safe so far." He turned to look at me. "No power out there. Sorry."

I said, "I bet it beats where I slept the last couple of nights." I told them about my adventures of the last two nights, and they told us how they outsmarted and overpowered their two assailants and how they wouldn't be coming for them. Ever.

I told them, "I really don't understand how your fellow soldiers would do that to you. I mean, they had to know you'd fight for your lives, right?"

Eddie only said, "They found out."

"I'm starving, by the way. I can't believe the gas station didn't have any snacks. Any chance you've got some food up there?" I was hoping he'd say he tricked it out like his greenhouse.

Wayne said, "As long as you can hunt, you can eat."

Dang it. "Have at it. Shoot something on the way so we can cook it when we arrive."

Eddie nudged me. "Somebody's hangry."

Eddie leaned over until our shoulders touched and squeezed my knee. "I can't believe parties unrelated leveled the house and Roger was there to scoop you up. That is one lucky bastard. Think about it. How does that happen? I'm sorry, Rae."

I squeezed his knee back. "We just have to hope his luck runs out before ours."

No one was behind us or in front of us for miles. We turned into a field that Wayne promised led to his land. He pointed to where Ritt should drive as we climbed up the sloped hill. At the crest, he told him to veer left and head toward the trees. Beyond the clump, I saw a shack and groaned. Beyond that, there was a larger and equally unappealing structure. I wasn't spoiled, but damn, a warm bed would be comforting tonight.

They wandered off to pee as soon as we got out. I looked for an outhouse and guessed I'd be squatting in the bushes later. Wayne yelled for me to go inside. "It's open."

I walked around the house and found a gaping hole instead of a door. I yelled back, "It's definitely open." It looked like a buffalo had run through it. I waited for the guys to catch up before stepping inside. Wayne cursed and cursed some more when he saw all the damage. It looked like an entire herd of them had been inside, wreaking havoc and pooping everywhere. The smell was so strong it took your breath away.

Outside, I asked, "What's Plan B?" Eddie asked what was the nearest town and suggested we go there. We got back on the paved road headed to Meeteestse. We drove straight to the Inn and checked into two rooms. Eddie and I stayed behind while they shopped for food. "I need a shower and some clean clothes."

Eddie pithily said, "Well, I need my rifle and a lot of ammo if I'm going to kill your uncle." I sat opposite him on the other double bed and swatted his knee.

"Eddie, I've told you a million times. It will never be your fault when I die. It will be my past and my family, such as it is. I know it's your nature to be this way. Remember this conversation if anything happens to me. And know that I'd rather it be me than you."

In the bathroom, I filled the sink with soapy water and washed my underwear, socks and t-shirt. After I took a shower, I washed my pants and sweatshirt in the tub and hung everything up over the shower curtain rod. Now if I could only get food. Eddie was on the phone when I checked for their return. I took advantage of the wait to blow-dry my underwear, bra, and t-shirt.

After I scarfed my food down, I continued drying my clothes. Having pants on was pretty essential at this point. Especially when being hunted. I turned my pants and pant pockets inside out to dry them from the inside and heard a clinking on the tub surface. After digging in the rocks, it surprised me that was all I had in my clothes. While sifting through debris, I uncovered a non-rock object. It was small, tubular and not organic. I held it up to the light and called Eddie in to inspect at it. I got dressed as he took it from me. "It was in my pants. Is it?" He nodded yes, put it on the floor and just as his foot was ready to stomp it, he stopped. He stared down at it. I knocked on his head. "What are you doing? Break it so he can't track us."

He suggested, "Perhaps we make him believe he's following you directly to this room."

I sat on the closed lid of the toilet. "We're sitting ducks here, Eddie. He could throw a rocket launcher in the window and that's the end of us."

He shook his head. "He can't actually throw one of those."

I stood up and pleaded, "Let's get out of here. It seems like my stomach is about to come up in throat."

He motioned for me to be quiet and placed the chip we found on the sink. "Don't touch it."

He sent Mickey a text before he called Wayne to come to our room. "Stay with her. Shoot through the door if anyone comes." Eddie promised to return quickly with new clothes in case there were additional trackers missed. I briefed Wayne on the situation, and he requested I remain in the bathroom while he kept watch at the window.

Eddie was back in five minutes and threw some clothes at me. "I raided the donation box." He looked up and said, "Lord, forgive me, it's for a good cause." I stripped down and redressed, commando style. I was itching already, thinking about what might be on the clothes. He gave me a choice of shoes: size 10 men's sneakers, size 8 platform sandals or size 9 Sperry loafers. Choosing the loafers, I grabbed the sneakers as a backup.

Ritt pulled his truck up to our door, and we jumped into the backseat. Instead of leaving town, Eddie wanted to go sit in the parking lot, kitty-corner to the inn. The heavily tinted backseat windows made it difficult to see at night. A car pulled up next to us and sat facing the inn like we were. He didn't get out. I had a dreadful sense it was Roger. Eddie and I crouched down, out of sight. He asked Wayne to feign taking a leak behind the truck. "Try to see the driver."

He came back and reported, "All I saw was a large male."

"Obviously, he doesn't know how you're traveling." Offered Ritt as we drove away.

"Pull over here." Snapped Eddie. "We've got to be sure it's him." He grabbed the shotgun, checked his shell count and asked what else was in the truck. Ritt offered his SIG

Sauer and .38 revolver he kept in the console. He grabbed
the SIG and shotgun, then instructed them to escort me to
Cody airport where the team was arriving. Wayne offered to
stay with him, but he wanted them both with me.

"Why don't we all stay? I don't want to leave you here."
I pulled on his sleeve and said, "Strength in numbers, and all
that. Let's plan this out so we can stay together."

While we deliberated, Ritt said, "Get down, lights coming
up behind us." The car we thought was his drove on until its
taillights disappeared. Wayne asked, "What are we thinking?
He wasn't going toward Cody if that's where we need to be."
I was aware of Eddie's intentions, but he wasn't equipped
adequately. He was prepared to face him alone to end my
nightmare.

I suggested, "Go to Cody. We need more guns, right? You
can never have enough. Isn't that what you say?"

Eddie finally agreed, making Ritt do a U-turn to travel
north. "Should only take about thirty minutes. And he thinks
you're in that room."

I kept looking for other cars and wondered, "Where is
everyone?"

The front seat riders laughed. "This state is the least
populated. No traffic jams to worry about here. No traffic is
a good thing." Despite its positives, bears make this state a
hard pass for me. One run in and I'm scarred for life.

We pulled into the airport and walked inside the terminal
without weapons, of course. I found the nearest tourist shop
and bought new clothes. No underwear yet, but my leggings
were brand new and untouched. I threw my stolen charity
clothes in the trash as I left the bathroom.

I saw Joe and the guys coming down the escalator and ran
to them. I jumped on Joe, wrapping my legs and arms around
him. He didn't even break stride as he handed his bag off to

Bobby and carried me out of the airport. Across the pickup lanes, he strode into short-term parking. There, he set me down and examined me, not to grope, but to ensure no injuries. I loathed it. I grabbed his hands and said, "I'm fine, just look at me." His Adam's apple bobbed and his jaw clenched as he pulled me in tight to smother me in his chest. His hug told me he loved me, was relieved, angry and determined. I looked up at him and said, "Joe, we're ending this here. I'm sure of it." He kissed my forehead and covered my head with his big paw.

We waited in the rental car area for them to get two SUVs. Joe asked if our new friends were up for the challenge of exterminating our biggest threat. They shook Joe's hand and said, "Whatever it takes, man." If it was Roger outside the Inn, he'd come back to check the GPS chip we left in the room and we'd be ready for him Our three-car caravan drove back toward the Inn, stopping at a hardware store to buy saws and drills. Wayne and Ritt returned to their room and took out a portion of the wall between theirs and ours for access if Uncle Roger entered. Wearing a hood, and bent over to disguise his size, Dusty rented the neighboring room and created a hole in the wall. The bathroom had small ventilation windows, leaving the front door as the sole entrance. Imagine his surprise, getting attacked from both sides of the room. I'll imagine him being blown to hell.

The old Inn would suffer from unwelcome renovations and likely endure significant damage. The stains already on the carpet would be insignificant. I hope there will be more stains with my relative's DNA.

You can easily run from one end of this town to the other without losing your breath. Places to hide meant getting up on a roof or in a tree. At almost midnight, the town was dark, except for the cowboy bar.

Roger knew everyone's profile in FETCH since he already encountered them, several times, nearly killing Jeff and Mickey. They weren't able to wander around town without becoming targets. GPS said I should be in the room, if he believed it. Once inside, Dusty moved it around the room to simulate my movements. I wondered if he was tracking it or simply waiting for me to leave so he could shoot me?

Rocky and Alex hid behind the first building as you enter town so they could see the traffic coming in. Mickey, Joe and I sat in the SUV in the bar parking lot. I reclined my seat when the bar closed to stay out of prying eyes and fell asleep.

DAY THIRTY

I woke up to Joe talking to the team. "There are too many civilians around here. Let's move this away from here. Dusty, grab the GPS and let's go."

Mickey said, "I'll inform the owners we'll pay for damage." Wayne and Ritt were tasked with discreetly returning to Dubois before us, acting inconspicuously, and serving as our informants in town. We gave them a fifteen-minute head start and followed the same route.

I expected a plane to land on us, or a passing truck to hit us or a torpedo to shoot us off the road as we drove. A wave of impending doom and defeat washed over me as I swiped a stray tear. Joe surprised me by telling me, "Knock it off. Pay attention and be ready. Today is the day this chapter ends."

I needed the kick in the pants. I repositioned myself and said, "Yes, sir." Positive affirmations flowed through me until we hit the city limits. Positive that we'd kill Roger today. Not sure if that counts spiritually, but it counts physically.

Wayne texted they were in the diner with all the regular customers and asked about their next move. Joe replied, "Go about your regular business. It would help if you could stay nearby and act as an extra set of eyes without drawing attention."

Mickey handed me two units as big as orzo pasta, one was Roger's GPS, one was ours. "Now the hard part. See if you can draw him out." Joe bent his head down when Mickey said that. I'll go to my grave hating myself if it's the last time I see him. I opened the door and got out with Joe yelling my name as I walked away.

I was so scared I forgot how to walk normally, like my brain was like, hey, a million eyes are on you, looking at your walk and your butt and probably your hair. Talk about random anxiety. I window shopped along the way to the diner. Why not die with a full stomach? I entered and located a table, away from windows, by the kitchen door. I walked past our new friends who sat up front today. After I ordered breakfast, I ambled to the bathroom to wash up. I stared at the mirror and prayed Roger wouldn't take a head shot and that he'd leave the team alone once I was dead. Cold water washed away my tears and sent me back to the table.

My nails still had dirt under them even after all the washing I'd done, so I turned sideways in my chair and under the table I used a toothpick to clean under them. Wanting to write Joe a farewell letter on the menu, I stood up and headed to ask for a pen.

The cook opened the kitchen door directly in front of me and stood with his arms outstretched. Uncle Roger stood behind him with a knife. He motioned me forward and pointed the knife at the cook. When I didn't move, he put his hand over the cook's mouth and stabbed him in the side. I darted toward him and followed as he held the cook in front of him and backed up, leading me into the kitchen, out of sight.

"Come with me or I'll slit his throat." The poor man's eyes pleaded with me as he held his bloody side. I shook my head yes and kept walking. This guy shouldn't die because of me.

"Ok, I'm following you. Now let him walk past me and leave."

He kept pulling him backward towards the door. Upon looking in the pass-through for her order, the waitress screamed at the sight of the cook's condition. Chairs scraped on the floor as people got up fast after she screamed. The door behind me banged open. Wayne and Ritt rushed inside and stopped behind me in the galley kitchen. Roger made a split-second decision to stab the cook again, then pushed him forward into my arms as he ran out the back door. Despite one of them firing a shot, the cook and I blocked them from following him out the door. They dragged the cook out from the galley-style kitchen while yelling for someone to call 911. They split up, exiting through both the front and back doors.

Before trailing Ritt, I cautiously peered out the back door. Joe grabbed me from behind and yelled, "Where the fuck is your comm?"

I reached up to my ear and remembered I took it off at the sink to wash my face. His face scared me into a mouth gaping mime. He lifted my shirt up enough to see the blood wasn't mine, and his chest heaved. The intensity that he bore through me made me shrivel up. "I'm sorry. I think I left it on the sink." He swiped his hand sideways and knocked utensils flying to the floor. Wayne let other people tend to the cook's non-life-threatening wounds while the rest of the diners watched them outside the kitchen door.

Joe said, "On my six. Tight." Waving his hand where I was supposed to be, we walked out the front door where the SUV waited for us. He yanked open the back door and steered me in with a push. His forceful slam could have amputated my foot if I hadn't fully withdrawn it. He launched himself into the front seat, then commanded,

"Drive." Rocky sped away from the diner going west. Joe called, "Report." Mickey, sitting next to me in the back, saw my empty ear and slyly handed me another comm. My face was fiery with embarrassment and the ringing in my ears made me deaf to their conversation. I royally fucked this up. Roger would be dead by now if I kept that comm in my ear. How could I be so careless?

Mickey was scanning drone images and told Rocky to punch it. "He's changed vehicles again."

We drove by a woman standing in the road, clutching her purse, waving us down. "Tell Wayne to stop and check her story. Get her plate number and issue a BOLO." Joe was calm as he added for Mickey to see if any local departments were available to assist with locating Roger. "Make sure you add armed and dangerous. Kill on sight."

The sound of the revved engine kept feeding my nerves and amping up my heart rate. The pulse in my temples throbbed, and I hated knowing I was the weakest link. Regardless, I was determined to be the one to bring this to an end. He was my problem. I watched my fingers as I touched each one to my thumbs repeatedly until I reached homeostasis.

Mickey said, "Turn off the road here. There's a dust trail going off the road."

I raised my head out of my self-recrimination and said, "This is Wayne's driveway. They blew his house up, but under the greenhouse is a bunker. He built tunnels that come up in two different directions, one in the field, one under the house."

At the last clearing, we spotted a car parked by the house's remains. Joe gave orders for spreading out, watching for cross fire and keeping our heads low. He instructed Mickey to back down the driveway, watch the drone, and stay alert for Roger.

Mickey touched his neck where Roger cut him last year and said, "You don't need to tell me twice."

Joe handed me two pistols and ammo clips and pulled my chin up to meet his eyes. "You stay on me like white on rice." He tersely kissed me, then we tried to find cover as we walked toward the house. Mickey reported no movement from Roger and for Eddie to move further north, and Rocky east to make our search grid equal.

I tugged on Joe's shirt and said, "Let's get in the greenhouse. We can come up where he won't expect." Joe agreed and told everyone to stay clear of that area. If we got followed in there, he was going to shoot, sight unseen.

Joe carefully cleared the greenhouse, looking behind the plastic partitions and pallets stacked against the back wall. Just as I moved a planter from over the trapdoor, Mickey said he saw movement low in the grass but didn't have positive ID it was Roger. I said to Joe, "Who the hell else would it be?"

Eddie screamed in our ears, "Give me confirmation and I'll light up the hillside."

I slid down the stairs and Joe followed. He positioned the planter and bag of dirt closer to the door for improved concealment.

Despite knowing we were all here, Roger was willing to risk his life to kill me. To have my death be his last dead. I was willing for his death to mine as well.

The greenhouse floor creaked when he entered it. His footsteps cleared it the same way Joe did when we walked in. He stopped over the door, weight shifting as he stood on it, probably contemplating his next move. We backed into the tunnel, waiting for him to find us. I intended to ambush him upon his descent, but Joe sensed our need to escape the tunnel. I sprinted with my hands on the side of the tunnel, with Joe nearly overtaking me. The flashbang Roger threw down the tunnel echoed and illuminated it temporarily.

Once Joe reached the end of the tunnel, he questioned the whereabouts of Roger. No one answered. Too much interference for the comms. Joe climbed the stairs with his gun leading the way. Tentatively, he pushed up on the door hatch to get a glimpse outside. He scanned the area for movement in case Roger had gone outside to wait for our exit. With his head partially out, he clicked for Mickey once more.

Two quick thudding gun shots hit very close to our position at the end of the tunnel. Joe jumped down the stairs and pushed me to the floor to cover me. I forgot to breathe until I let out a gasp. He told me to stay low and behind him as we crept back toward the greenhouse. We could see a body sprawled before us in the light streaming from the open trapdoor.

Blood poured from the man's head as he lay face down. Joe kicked the gun away from his body before he turned him over. I pushed Joe to the side so I could see for myself. A final death twitch scared me into putting another bullet, or three into his chest. Uncle Roger's eyes stayed open, even after his last breath. Joe took my hand and pulled me toward the exit.

In the greenhouse, Joe called the team to gather, giving the all clear. Joe confirmed Roger was dead and asked Dusty and Rocky to go pull his body out of the tunnel. That's when I lost it. I fell to the floor and blubbered. My tears and noise expelled the fear and hatred I held for him, leaving only freedom and gratitude. He was definitely dead. Joe helped me up and embraced me as if it were a new beginning. The relief and victory on the guys' faces told me it was a big deal for them, too.

They pulled his body up the stairs and laid him outside the greenhouse. Observing the hole in his head, FETCH exchanged looks, inquiring about the gunshot wounds I caused in his chest. They treated him like a crime scene and took photos, prints, blood and hair samples.

Joe said, "I appreciate the backup, and I hate to ask, but who disobeyed orders and came down the tunnel?" They all proclaimed innocence. He gave a quick look to Mickey, hoping he would disclose the information, but Mickey denied seeing anyone enter.

"Is it possible that someone was already in the tunnel beneath the house?" I wondered out loud. Eddie ventured back into the tunnel to see where it led as we stood watching Alex get samples.

Eddie yelled to us from his exit point. According to him, he emerged in the shed initially, then proceeded through the tunnel during the early stages of construction to the back corner of the now fallen house, and climbed the stairs indented in the dirt. We must've missed the hidden tunnel when we were there. He looked confused about that detail. He said, "Guess Wayne didn't tell us about that leg of the tunnel."

Joe said, "Let's go look at your drone." He eyed Eddie suspiciously but said to everyone, "Last chance, I'm not mad. You saved our asses. You showed up just in time." Still, no one came forward. As we approached the truck to retrieve Mickey's computer, we discovered the door was open, and the computer was missing.

Mickey swore while he searched under his seat and even in the back seat. "Tell me now before I wipe out a bunch of files that, needless to say, no one else needs to see." No one stopped him as he got out his phone and ran a program to disable his computer. He explained each function he wiped out, though none of understood. We stared at each other, seeking a guilty or proud expression, curious about the identity of our guardian angel.

I was hoping beyond reality for a miracle. "Maybe it was my dad. Or the guy that picked me up in Chenango Forks. Maybe JD knows."

Joe pulled me tight against his side and said, "We'll figure it out."

Bobby inquired, "Shall we conduct an autopsy for ballistics or incinerate him on the spot?"

Alex said he got all his samples for DNA before we voted to cremate him. Although Joe really wanted to determine who made the kill shot, he finally agreed.

They made a border around his body in the stone driveway so the fire wouldn't escape and destroy anything except him. Then checked his clothing for explodables and took his boots off. Guess they wanted him crispy all the way to his toes. They covered him with branches, doused him with gas from the ATVs, and lit the makeshift crematory on fire.

I clung to Joe as relieved tears slid down my cheeks. The enormity of my uncle's death left my body in waves as we watched his body being reduced to bones and dust. The evil threat that was Roger rose to the sky in changing colors of brown to gray to black and finally to white. It was disgusting and yet cathartic.

We stood, silently mesmerized by the lingering smoke until Mickey threw a small boulder on top of his bones. Roger had almost killed him, so his death must have been a solid victory for him. The other guys picked up rocks and piled them on with vigor.

Eddie handed me a sizeable rock and said, "Last one."

I held it and mused, "I'm so happy there won't be a next time for him, because this time was definitely his last time." I raised the rock with two hands above my head and slammed it onto his rocky grave.

THE END

In honor of Michelle Goddess. Her ability to brighten the lives of others through her generosity, encouragement, and support was truly extraordinary. Her legacy of giving carried on in death through organ donation, enabling others to keep shining.

In memory of our beagle, Betty Lou. Cancer may have shortened her life, but her warrior spirit and zest for life inspired us to be better humans.

To my husband, Tom. He remains everything I need.

To my family and friends who enrich my life. My mother, Patricia Ross, who is the kindest woman I've ever met. My friends, my tribe of women: Nancy Acker, Jodi Dresmich, Denice Hartmann, Phyllis Felker, Barbara Gunnells, Donna Moffitt, Jean Pemberton, Janet Ross, Judy Smith and Amy Young.

To Wendi Lee and Stacy Diffendorf for their computer skills and helping with the hard stuff.